The Valley and the Shadow

a novel of loss and hope

Tony Myers

Romans 11:29

Tony Myers

1

The Valley and the Shadow

www.tonymyers.net

A note to the reader:

Thank you for picking up this book. It is a book about loss, specifically the loss of a child. Like all my books, it has elements of a suspense mystery. It's also adventurous in nature, but my hope is that the elements of the story do not deter from the fact that it is a fictional book about the loss of a child.

Please note that I have written this book as a father who has been through the loss of a baby girl. Our firstborn, Alethia Joy, died when my wife was 39 weeks pregnant. She was stillborn. If you are currently suffering from the loss of a child, please remember as you read the book that I have been through it myself.

The story you are about to read is not my story. Though there are similarities to how I felt at times, ultimately this is a story about a fictional father and mother. My hope is that their story can help others work through their own suffering and maybe find a glimmer of hope in the process.

Know that I will be praying for you as read this book. Please don't hesitate to contact me through my website or through social media and let me know how I can be praying for you more specifically.

Sincerely, Tony Myers

@tony1myers (twitter)

www.tonymyers.net

Acknowledgments

I must start off saying "thank you" to a number of people. When I think of people who have helped contribute to this book, it also makes me think of others who have influenced my life. People have inspired me and encouraged me along life's road, and how can I not say "thank you" to everyone who's played a positive part in my life. I'm the person I am today because of so many people. Thank you all!

As always, I want to thank my wife. First of all, for just being by my side these twelve plus years. It's been quite a journey, and I have no idea what the future holds. It should be exciting. I love you so much. More directly, thank you for looking over the manuscript and proofreading it. I don't know what I'd do without you.

A big thank you to Stephen for once again, giving the manuscript an edit. I really, really appreciate it. In your honor... "Go Penguins!"

I definitely have to thank my late grandfather, Ron Duranske. He truly was a skilled fisherman and a provider for others. He had many adventures in his life, and I wouldn't be surprised to discover that aspects of this story may have happened in his life. His legacy lives on. Also, thank you to Uncle Sean for agreeing to be in the book. I hope the story brought back some fond memories.

My wife's grandparents, Milo and Gladys, also receive a big "thank you." I enjoyed putting them in the story; but, even more than that, I'm thankful that they truly have cared for people and helped many others. Though this story is fiction, their care for others is not.

Thinking back to the time my wife and I went through the loss of our little girl, Alethia, I couldn't help but think of our church, Cornerstone Bible Church. As we endured the deepest trial of our lives, our church couldn't have done a better job of walking with us through that valley. In many regards it was a "small country church," but its impact was huge both in our life and in the lives of others.

Thank you to Hannah Beth, Anthony, Elliot, and Autumn Joy. You help to make each day a little brighter. Love you guys so much!

Lastly, I give glory to God for all He's done. We've been given so much. I'm thankful for His Son, the Good Shepherd, Jesus Christ, who walks through life with us. He was even with us when we passed through the valley of the shadow of death. All these stories are ultimately His.

❧❧

To Alethia Joy,

We will never forget you.

❧❧

Character Index

Damien Parker - Businessman from North Carolina in his early thirties, part-owner in *Parker & Wheaton Marketing Services,* ex-Marine, African-American in nationality, married to Julia

Henry Wheaton – Part-owner of *Parker & Wheaton Marketing Services,* in his late sixties, widower

Julia Parker – Wife of Damien, from Georgia, home maker

Rufus - Lawyer for *Parker & Wheaton Marketing Services,* late twenties, likes to party

Lex Williamson – Owner of *Worldwide Pathways Incorporated,* in his mid-seventies, walks with a cane

Captain Jones – Ferry driver from the island of St. Kitts to Nevis, in his mid-fifties

Ron – Fisherman in his early seventies, ex-Navy officer

Sean – Ron's son-in-law, Asian descent

Elizabeth – Nurse from St. Kitts, well known by the people of St. Kitts for her poverty to success story, married with a ten-year-old son

Beck – Surfer with shaggy blond hair, in his early twenties

Milo – Preacher in his late seventies, many years of being a pastor, married to Gladys

Gladys – Senior woman in her late seventies, married to Milo

Ned – American businessman

Zack Smithson - Young pilot, runs a small charter plane as a small business

Map of St. Kitts & Nevis

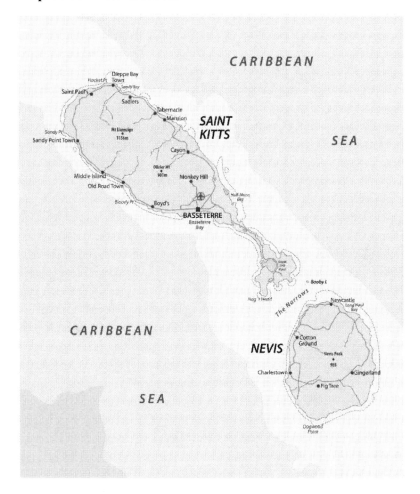

Prologue

Damien Parker sat quietly watching the people in the crowded cafeteria. Some were sad. Others were filled with joy. Many seemed indifferent. He wondered where they were going once they left. He no longer looked at people simply as a means to an end. He had always heard the famous quote by Shakespeare, but now he truly believed it, "All the world's a stage, and all the men and women merely players." Each of these people had a story. Some would tell stories of defeat and hopelessness, while others would tell of triumph and victories in their lives. A part of Damien wished he could've stopped every one of them and heard each of their stories.

He was an affluent African-American businessman, who had interacted with many people through various contacts at home and abroad. Many people would cross his path each year, and too often he never found out much about them, other than what he needed to know for business. At times Damien wished he could relive many of those past years of his life. He desired to go back and interact with people on a deeper level in order to find out their stories. He knew this could never happen. He couldn't change who he had been in the past. It was sealed and now a part of his story.

Damien grew up in the small town of Wake Forest, North Carolina. He was the only child of his father and mother. They were faithful churchgoers, always present whenever the doors were open. His parents were some of the few Lutherans in a town filled with Baptists. Religion had always been a part of Damien's life. Even as he grew older and joined the Marines, he found himself around those that kept faith as a central part of their lives. Looking back, he was thankful for this. He tended to have a wild side about him, and his comrades were usually there to keep him on the straight and narrow when he started to veer off the path.

His mother had passed away during his time in basic training. It was truly a difficult time in his life. He'd always been close to her and she was an inspiration to him in everything. She gave her whole heart to her family. Damien had always known that no matter where he went and what he did, he was never too far from her heart and mind. Even during his wild streak in high school, he knew that his mother's rules and admonitions were spoken out of love. More than ever, he wished he could tell her how much he appreciated those corrective talks.

After serving four years in the Marines, Damien went back to school part-time and pursued a degree in business marketing. Like anything else he did, he excelled in his studies, and at the age of twenty-four, he started working for a small but upcoming marketing firm, Wheaton Strategies. He worked hard and quickly made his way up the chain of command, until he was brought on as a partner in the business. The company's name was then changed to *Parker & Wheaton Marketing Services*. They had arisen to become a multi-million-dollar company that had dealings internationally. They were able to do this with less than twenty-five employees.

While studying for his marketing degree, he met a young lady named Julia Overton, who was now Julia Parker, his wife. She was a beautiful, white woman with light brown hair from Georgia. She was funny, brilliant, and strong— everything Damien wanted in a wife. They easily found commonality as they were two of the oldest students in their classes that were filled with mostly eighteen-year-olds. After simply ten months of dating, they were happily married. He thanked God that she was a part of his story.

Damien continued to watch the crowd as people passed by in a hurry. He had become much more pensive these last two years. He took a sip from the Styrofoam cup in front of him and gently placed it down on the table. The individual across the table spoke, "Is it time to go back?"

Out of habit Damien looked down at his wrist. He smiled to himself as there was nothing there. He nodded slightly as he spoke quietly, "Yes... it's time to go back."

15

Chapter 1

"Yes, that will be fine," Damien said into the phone. He stood with his carry-on bag over his shoulder in the Raleigh-Durham International airport. He was dressed formally in a khaki colored suit. He tried to keep his voice down, but he couldn't contain his excitement. This call could potentially lead to his company's biggest business deal ever.

"Are you sure three weeks isn't too soon?" the voice on the line asked.

"No sir. I know we can make this happen."

"Very well. I guess we will see you then. You let me know if anything comes up, and I'll inform the company that you and Mr. Wheaton plan on being here in three weeks."

"I look forward to it, and likewise, let me know if anything comes up from your end."

"Sounds good, goodbye for now."

"Goodbye," Damien said as he ended the phone call. He pumped his fist and let out a quick shout, "Yeah, baby!" A few people nearby turned and stared at this well-dressed businessman giddy with excitement. Usually he was a sight to see in and of himself, being a muscular, 6'4" man who typically dressed in high class suits. Folks occasionally approached him and asked if he played in the NBA or NFL. Oftentimes people would say he resembled either Dwayne Wade or Cam Newton.

The meeting he had just set up was with an international company stationed in Portugal. It dealt with imports and exports out of Central American countries. He had been working on this contract for a long time. It sounded very promising that a deal would be struck. They now had a scheduled meeting set up in three weeks on the small island of Nevis southeast of St. Kitts.

Passing a flower stand, he stopped to buy a flower for his wife, Julia. She was at home, nine months pregnant. She hadn't felt the greatest lately. The hot temperatures of the past summer months had really taken their toll on her, and she was waiting anxiously for the young one to arrive. They found out the gender of their baby as soon as they could, and both were excited when they heard that a beautiful baby girl was on the way. The due date was only five days away, and they were eagerly counting down the days until they would meet the newest member of their family.

"This one will do," Damien said, grabbing a white rose. The sales clerk smiled and typed the appropriate code into the register. The price on the register came to nine dollars and some change.

Damien quickly paid the clerk, who mumbled the words, "Thank you." Damien smiled in return and continued toward the exit of the airport. He knew this place well. In many regards he felt like the RDU airport was his office. He easily flew out from here an average of two or three times a month.

Reaching the long-term parking, Damien headed toward his car. He always parked in the premium section as he didn't want anything to happen to his custom Dodge Viper. His car was on one of the top levels of the parking deck, and he decided to take the elevator up. He could have easily called for a valet, but today he would enjoy the walk. It would give him more time to think of the meeting he had just set up with this international shipping company.

Stepping into the elevator, he felt his phone buzz. Pulling it out he could see that the notification was from an app he had recently downloaded. It was one that delivered to him a Bible verse for the day. He smiled as he read the verse, Psalm 23:2, "The LORD makes me to lie down in green pastures. He leads me beside the still waters." He couldn't help but laugh to himself. *Oh yes, he's leading me to some green pastures,* Damien thought. *Green pastures of money after I close this next deal.* Things were going well. The future was bright.

৵৽৽

Damien drove east on Interstate 40, weaving through traffic. The V-8 motor in his Viper sounded like a thing of beauty. It easily accelerated as Damien shifted gears. He had received many tickets in his days, which he only saw as a small bump in the road. They were well worth the price he would pay to drive the way he wanted when he wanted. A few years back, a judge threatened to strip him of his license for a year. It was then that he made a rule for himself to try to keep it under ten over the speed limit.

Looking down at his dashboard, he tapped a button on his phone to call Henry Wheaton, his business partner. It was just after five in the afternoon. Surely Henry Wheaton would still be at the office at this time of day. The phone rang three times before Henry picked up, "Hello."

"Henry, how ya' doing, my friend?" Damien said with excitement clearly in his voice.

"I'm doing well, Damien. By the tone of your voice, I take it things went well in Houston," Henry said, trying to get right down to business.

"Yeah, Houston was fine, no surprises there, but listen—I've got something that will easily overshadow anything else we're doing."

"Oh… don't tell me you're playing the lottery again."

"Haha, no way, man. You know that deal we've been working on with *Worldwide Pathways Incorporated,* stationed in Portugal?"

"Yes, the one that fizzled earlier this year."

A smile formed on Damien's face as he was excited for what he was about to tell his longtime friend. "Well, that's long in the past. I spoke to their CEO and they're interested in doing a deal with us."

Henry was a little confused by Damien's excitement. "Parker, that sounds good, but isn't this a small account? Don't they simply ship goods between west Africa and Europe?"

"That's what I first thought," Damien replied as he continued to weave through traffic. "It turns out that those are just their main shipping ports. These guys actually have dealings all up and down the whole east coast as well as Central America and southern Florida. It's a lot bigger than we realized. We're talking millions and millions of dollars in assets."

Henry sat in silence for a moment, trying to take in what Damien was saying. Being close to seventy, he had overseen many business dealings over the years, and he knew when something sounded off and a little too good to be true. He was a man of wisdom, and though he wasn't very affectionate, he was known for his kindness in looking out for the needs of his employees as well as through serving various charities. Sometimes Damien would get upset with his apprehension to close some of their deals. Henry liked to check and double check everything before it was all said and done.

He spoke with great caution in his voice. "Damien... something doesn't sound quite right." He paused for a moment before continuing, "Don't you think we would've found out about their broad transactions in our initial research into this company?"

Damien laughed a little at Henry's response. "You're becoming soft, old man."

Henry quickly objected. "Hey, who're you calling soft? Don't forget, I can still easily beat you in arm wrestling." The two men had always had a good relationship and had never had an angry argument in all their four years of being partners.

"Haha, keep dreaming. Listen, talking with their rep, they think they can grow their market in these places. He said others aren't able to deliver like they are. There is much room to expand if we can target the right audience in our marketing."

Henry took a deep breath, trying to think through everything Damien was saying. "I don't know, Parker. Something doesn't sound like it's adding up."

"All right, how 'bout this. We have a meeting scheduled in three weeks on the island of Nevis. You come with me on this one, and bring Rufus."

"Three weeks! You've got a baby coming. Are you sure you're going to be ready by then?"

"Haha, look man, I've been through basic training. As Marines we're supposed to be ready for anything." Damien paused for moment, changing his tone. "In all seriousness, it's looking like the baby will be here in just a few days anyway."

Henry chuckled slightly, "Well, don't hold your breath, my friend. Those young ones tend to come on their own schedule."

"I hear ya'. So, is that a yes?"

Henry paused for a moment, thinking everything through. He knew that the meeting on Nevis was a good idea to be sure everything was in order before a deal was made. "Ok, Damien, you just worry about that new baby of yours. Send me all the info via email and make sure everything is set up."

"Thanks, Henry. You have a good night, and be sure to head home before it gets too late."

"All right... see you later," he said, hanging up the phone.

Damien was excited that Henry was now informed about the meeting in Nevis. Though Damien often made jokes and jabs at his business partner, he truly appreciated him. Henry had taken him under his wing when he started working at the company. He had trusted Damien with many responsibilities early on, and gave him the freedom to pursue new accounts on his own. Above and beyond all that, Henry had brought him on as a partner after simply four years of working under him. Henry's wife had passed away not long before Damien started working for the company, and Damien always wondered if their relationship helped to fill a void in the midst of Henry's loss. He would never know for sure, but nevertheless he would be forever grateful for all Henry had done for him.

Damien pulled into the driveway of his large home in Cary, North Carolina, just west of Raleigh. The house was a two-story brick home with well-tilled landscaping around it. Between him and his wife, they had plenty of space for themselves, and plenty of room for their new child to grow up. He looked forward to the day when his daughter would come running out the front door, excited for his return home.

He parked his car in the garage, grabbed the flower, and quickly headed inside. This was one of his shorter trips as he had only been gone a couple of days. "Hey Babe, I'm home," he announced as he opened the door.

"I'm here, Damien," Julia said, with obvious fatigue in her voice. He walked toward the sound of her voice and found her stirring a pot on the stove. He smiled as he saw her. She looked tired. It was obvious that she was feeling more and more uncomfortable as her due date approached. Her brown hair was pulled back in a ponytail, and she was dressed casually, still in her pajama pants.

"Hey," Damien said, walking over and giving her a kiss. "How're you feeling?"

"I'm ok... Just happy you're home," she said, smiling at her husband. She then took notice of the rose. "Is that for me?"

"Of course, Babe," he said, holding the white rose out to his wife. She gently grabbed it out of Damien's hand and held it to her nose. She leaned back against the counter. It was obvious that she was tired from being on her feet all day, making preparations for the baby's arrival.

Damien gently patted her pregnant belly. "No baby yet I guess."

Julia set the flower aside before speaking up. "No... but trust me, you will be the first to know."

Damien laughed before continuing. "How did your doctor's appointment go yesterday?"

"Fine. Nothing new, just waiting on baby."

"No slight contractions or anything like that?"

Julia shook her head. "No, but he did say that he wouldn't let me go too far past my due date."

Damien nodded as he spoke, "Well, I'm glad to hear everything's still going well and the baby didn't decide to come early."

Julia smiled as she continued to stir the pot. It looked to be a simple meal of pasta with vegetables. This meal was her comfort food during these last months of pregnancy. "How did things go in Houston?" she said quietly.

Damien rested his back against the counter and crossed his arms. He had a lot to tell his wife. "Houston went fine. Negotiations were quick. The deal closed without any major issues."

"Great to hear," Julia sighed, her voice full of fatigue.

"But, listen, there's something else. I finally got a call back from a deal I've been working on for a while now."

"Which one was that?"

Damien couldn't hide his smile. "Do you remember a few months back when I was trying to work a deal with a company called *Worldwide Pathways Incorporated*?"

"I think so," Julia said, trying to search her memory. "Are they the ones that run a fleet of ships between Africa and Europe?"

"Yes, but that's not all," Damien continued, leaning forward and stepping closer to his wife. "It turns out that they've been known to run ships through the Caribbean, even all the way to Miami. It's a much bigger deal than even I anticipated."

"How big of a deal is this?"

His excitement was clearly on full display at this point. "We're talking in the millions. We'll most likely have to hire a small team just to assist with this new deal."

Any other time Julia would have matched his excitement, but the state of being nine months pregnant took a lot of her energy. "That's great, my love. It sounds like the kind of deal you've been waiting for. When do you close?"

"Ok." He took another step closer to his wife and gently placed his hands on her shoulders. "We plan to meet in the Caribbean in three weeks to close the deal."

"Three weeks," Julia echoed with just a bit of concern in her voice. "We'll probably have a two-week-old baby by then."

"I know... I know," Damien assured her, trying to speak as compassionately as he could. "And if you want me to push the meeting back a week or two then I can definitely do so. I just figured your mom should be here by that time, and things will be a little settled."

Julia went back to stirring the pasta, trying to process everything that was said. From Damien's perspective, she didn't look completely closed to the idea.

He continued, "Listen, I'll be in and out of there as quickly as I can. I figure with flight patterns, I'll only be gone two days total, and then I'll be..."

"No, I understand," Julia interrupted. "This is quite a big deal for you, and though I don't want you to be gone, I understand how huge this is for you and the company. And you're right, I should be fine with my mom here to help."

Damien smiled at his wife, thankful for her understanding. "You sure, Babe?"

She smiled back. "Yeah, I'm sure."

He wrapped his wife in his arms. He leaned his head against hers. "Thanks for understanding."

Chapter 2

Damien awoke early. It was a Saturday morning, and he was planning on getting a good start to the day. Their town of Cary had gotten some rain earlier in the week and the grass had grown quite a bit lately. They lived on a lot that was just under an acre and it took a considerable amount of time to mow. Damien didn't mind the work. He found it relaxing and a good change of pace from his normal busy schedule at the office.

Julia spoke as Damien sat up. "You're getting up early this morning."

He swung his feet off the side of the bed, and yawned as he spoke, "Yeah, the grass is getting a little high, and I'd better mow it before this little girl decides to come." He then looked back at his wife. "You want to help?" he said sarcastically.

Julia picked up a pillow and threw it at him. Damien laughed under his breath. He walked toward the bedroom window and pulled the curtains to the side. The sky was clear, and it appeared to be a good day to work on the yard. The grass needed mowing, the edges needed trimming, and there were weeds that needed to be pulled. He looked forward to tackling these jobs and getting them completed.

After a short stop in the bathroom, Damien changed into his work clothes and headed for the door. Realizing something was missing, he went back to the nightstand beside his bed and grabbed his watch. It was a high quality, silver, scratch resistant watch with a matching silver band. It was durable enough to be worn for any activity, but still was classy enough to be worn for formal events. He loved it, and only took it off when he was sleeping.

Damien noticed a small smudge on the glass. He walked to the nearby window to see more clearly. He gently rubbed it with his fingers, cleaning it off as best as he could. Light from the window gleamed off the face. It truly was a nice timepiece. He strapped it on his wrist as he walked back toward the door.

Going down the steps, a distant memory flooded his mind. The brief moment of admiring the watch had brought it back...

Damien arrived at the hospital and found his mother resting in bed. His father was at her bedside. Damien approached her as quietly as he could. She was resting peacefully. There was a nurse by his side. "It won't be long now," he heard her say quietly to his father.

Seeing his son, Damien's father arose from his seat and gave him a hug. "Thanks for coming, Son. I imagine it wasn't easy leaving basic training."

Damien nodded, fighting back the tears. "Yeah," he said under his breath. He and his mother had always been close. He couldn't believe she was facing the end.

His father gently rubbed his back to comfort him. "Son, why don't you take your time with her. I'll be out in the hall if you need anything."

"Right," Damien said quietly as his father turned to leave. He approached his mother who was in bed with her eyes closed. Although she was frail, strangely enough Damien thought she looked strong in that moment. The long battle with cancer had taken its toll on her body, but through it all she had shown she was a fighter.

Sensing Damien's presence, she opened her eyes. "Hello, Son," she said quietly as he sat beside her.

He grabbed her right hand with both hands before continuing to speak. "How are you feeling?"

"Not bad. The doctors are taking good care of me."

Damien nodded as he looked off to the side. Tears began to run down his cheeks.

His mother spoke up, seeing his tears, "Oh, Son, don't cry for me. I've made my peace with God, and as the Scriptures say, 'I will dwell in the house of the LORD forever.'"

"No, Mom, it's not that. I just… I just don't want to lose you," he said, squeezing her hand tighter.

"I know, Damien. There's a part of me that doesn't want to leave you. I wished more than anything that I could've seen you graduate from basic training. I would've loved to have seen you a full-fledged Marine. I'm sorry I can't hold on much longer."

Damien's tears turned into a sob. "No… Mom… no," he spoke through staggered speech, wiping his eyes as best as he could. "You've done… so much for me. I just… I love you."

"I love you too, Son," she said quietly. The two sat in silence for a few moments, trying to hold onto these moments as long as they could. They both recognized that this may be her last day on this earth. Neither of them knew exactly what they should say or do.

It was a few moments later that his mother spoke up, "Damien, I want you to look over to the side… on that table." Damien turned and saw a small box sitting on the table. It was wrapped in silver paper and had a bow on top. He reached for it and tried to hand it to his mother.

"No, I want you to have it," she said, gently pushing it away from herself.

"Mom, what is it?"

"Open it."

Damien took his time pulling off the bow. He was trying to savor every moment, knowing that this was the last gift he would ever receive from her. She had always been generous on Christmas and birthdays. Through her actions she had taught her son the joy of giving. Damien tore into the paper and could see it was a simple white box underneath. He carefully opened the lid and pulled out the silver watch that sat inside. It was a thing of beauty. Damien instantly fell in love with it.

His mother spoke quietly, "I bought it for your graduation, but I thought it best to give it to you now."

Damien sat admiring it, rubbing his thumb over the face. Even though he loved it, no words came to mind. His mother continued, "Go ahead, try it on."

Damien loosened the strap as he slid it on his wrist. It fit well. He looked at the second hand on the clock ticking away. Something about the watch looked different. He couldn't describe it, but he knew it was like no other watch he had ever seen before. It was mesmerizing. It would forever link him to this moment.

"Now, Damien," his mother said as she reached over and grabbed his arm. She had a stern look on her face. "Don't let this watch become a thing of bitterness. May it remind you of life, not death. I want it to be a thing of hope, not despair. I love you, Son. I want you to know that life is too short to live in anger and regret. Live it to the fullest. Live it with hope, peace, and love in your heart."

"Yes, Mom," he said as the tears continued to fall.

"Now come here, my boy, let me pray for you," she said, reaching out with her hand. Damien leaned forward as she placed her hand on the back of his head.

"Dear God, be with my son. Look after him and his father for me as I am going away. He needs your help, God. Help him to be strong. Help him to know that you are leading him in this life as the Good Shepherd. May he cling tightly to you, knowing that you can bless him and make his cup overflow. Thank you, God, for all you do for us. I pray these things in the name of the LORD Jesus Christ. Amen."

A simple watch, yet so full of memories. Damien was thankful that it was durable and could be worn everywhere. It reminded him of the hope his mother had in those final moments. In a way it was like his mother was always with him through anything he would encounter in this life. She had left a legacy for him, one he felt would live on and never die.

As he passed through the back door of his house, Damien felt the heat of the sun fall upon him. It was a beautiful day. He reached his small shed on the back end of his yard. He fiddled with the lock on the door as he turned to see his elderly neighbor already at work in his own backyard. "Good morning, Damien!" the man said.

"Hello, Fred!" he yelled back.

"How's your wife doing?"

Damien smiled as he yelled back, "She's doing well, holding strong!"

"I guess the baby ain't come yet?"

"No... no baby, yet... but I better get to work because it could be at any moment that the little lady plans on entering the world."

"Great idea, best wishes to you!"

"Thanks. You have a good day," Damien said as he opened the door in front of him. He was thankful for his neighborhood. He and Julia often commented that their neighborhood block captured the true essence of what an old-fashioned community was all about.

It was just a few minutes later that the mower was started, and Damien began the hour journey of cutting the grass. It felt a little strange to him, knowing that the next time he cut this grass, his little girl would be here. His dad used to give him tractor rides when he was a young boy. He couldn't wait to do the same for his little girl.

Julia, still in her nightgown, looked out the window as she saw her husband starting to mow. Sleep had eluded her. She was both nervous and excited for the baby to come. She wondered if today would be the day. Julia couldn't help but chuckle as her husband passed by the window again on the mower. He reminded her of a little boy excited to drive a tractor for the first time. It brought her much joy to see him take pleasure in something as simple as mowing the grass.

Julia walked across the hall to the baby's room. It was decorated in beautiful shades of purple and white. The crib was set up, along with a mobile dangling above where the baby would sleep. There was already a dresser with a changing pad on top. A few toys rested along one window sill. This time what really caught her eye amid everything was the rocking chair in the corner. Gazing at it, she dreamed of all the time she would spend nursing the baby and singing her to sleep. Those would be precious times; ones she felt like she could already see in her mind's eye.

As the morning wore on, Julia took her time getting ready. Damien continued to work on the yard all the way till lunchtime. Nothing was planned for the day as these days were kept open while they were waiting for the baby to arrive. Lunchtime was approaching, and Julia began getting things ready for a simple meal of sandwiches. The house was very quiet. She smiled as she thought of how these quiet days would soon come to an end with the birth of their little girl. She looked forward to the laughter and the crying that would soon fill the house.

The quietness of the house was interrupted as Damien came through the back door. He wiped his forehead as he entered the kitchen. "Whoa... Feels good in here." He stepped closer to where his wife was standing. "What's for lunch?"

"Nothing much. Just trying to finish up this leftover turkey from the other day."

Damien nodded his head as he leaned against the counter. He spoke casually, "Well, it's a sunny day outside. What do you say we take this meal outside and eat on the patio, in the shade of course?"

Julia looked up at the nearby window in the kitchen. It truly looked like a beautiful, peaceful day. As she was looking, a bird flew close and landed near the window. It was as if it was calling to her to come outside. She smiled back at her husband as she spoke, "I like that idea, but I'd say if we're going to have a picnic, let's do it right. This may be the last chance we get for just the two of us."

"So, what do you suggest?"

"Falls Park is not far. Let's get that picnic basket we got as a wedding gift and fill it up."

Damien laughed slightly. "I like it, Babe. I'll go get it."

❧

Damien and Julia sat comfortably on a checkered blanket out in an open field at the park. Their lunch was finished, and now they were just sitting back, reclining and talking like they always had since their first dates. They watched as kids played on a nearby playground, others walked their dogs, a father and son threw a frisbee, and many others just casually enjoyed the great outdoors.

Currently, the two were laughing at the thought of Damien changing a diaper—a feat he had never accomplished. Julia laughed as she talked. "On your first attempt I'm going to be sure the nurses take a few pictures of you trying to figure everything out."

Damien quickly countered, "No way, Babe. It will be just like one of our Marine missions. I'll assess the situation at hand, quickly plan it out and complete the given objective. End of story."

His wife laughed even harder as a few tears fell from the edges of her eyes. She had trouble talking while she was laughing so hard. "I would like... to see you try. You might... be over your head on this one, Mr. Marine."

"Well, like anything else, if there's a problem I'll call for backup."

Julia kept laughing. "I think you might need a team of Marines for this one."

The two continued to laugh and talk in the park as the minutes passed by. Their life had been such an adventure up to this point. They knew the coming of their little girl was going to be the biggest adventure yet. Julia was so thankful for her husband. He was beyond any ideal she ever had hoped for in a spouse. He was a provider, a leader for their family, but most of all, a good man. She loved him so much.

Damien changed their current conversation to a more serious topic. "You still thinking the same name for our girl?"

Julia was taken a little off guard by the sudden change in the conversation. She leaned over and grabbed her husband's hand. She smiled as she spoke. "Damien... yes. I think we should definitely name her Lucinda... after your mother."

"Are you sure? I mean Lucinda is a little old fashioned, don't you think?"

"I like it." Julia scooted a little closer to her husband. "And like I said before, we can call her Lucy. It's cute."

Damien looked away as he smiled. "Cute? I don't know about cute. Marines don't do cute."

Julia rolled her eyes. "Come on, be serious. It will be a good reminder of your mother you've always told me about."

Damien nodded in return as he gently rubbed his wife's stomach. "Well, I guess that settles it once and for all. She'll be our little Lucy."

"Thanks, my love," Julia said as she leaned over and gave her husband a kiss.

♥♥

The rest of the day was very relaxing as Damien and Julia spent the day together. The thought of having the name finalized seemed to make the arrival of their child an even greater reality. They spoke endlessly of what it would be like to raise her. They talked through dreams and plans they had for their young family. They would both admit that it was one of the best days they'd ever had as a married couple.

As Damien got ready for bed, he passed by the baby's room and took one more glance inside. He stood in the doorway and looked at his wife as she sat quietly rocking in the chair in the corner. It was a beautiful scene; one that he was thankful was going to become a regular sight in the Parker household.

"What are you doing, my love?" Damien asked.

Julia looked up and smiled at her husband. She gently patted her stomach as if the baby was already sleeping peacefully in her lap. She spoke quietly, "I already just love her so much, Damien... I love her so much."

Damien looked down at the floor as he smiled. He truly didn't know what to say in that moment. He just felt thankful. Thankful for everything God had given him. He looked up at his wife and simply said, "Goodnight, Julia... goodnight, Lucy... I love you both."

Chapter 3

Sunday morning began as it did every week. Damien awoke a little before seven and went downstairs. He had gone to bed early the night before and felt very refreshed this morning. The sun was starting to rise and the sunlight could be seen through the windows as he came to the bottom of the steps. He rubbed his eyes, trying to force the sleep from them. Their church didn't begin till ten o'clock, but out of habit he always rose early.

Inside the kitchen, the coffee pot waited for him to get things started. He reached into the cupboard for the coffee and found they were out of grounds. Damien sighed as he simply poured himself a glass of water. It did the trick to further wake him. He gently placed the glass in the sink and headed back up the steps to get ready for the morning.

As Damien started up the stairs, he stopped suddenly. He wasn't sure why he stopped, but he turned and took one last look out the front window. The sun was bright, everything was calm. *Peace* was the word that came to his mind. The weather was pleasant. He lived in a beautiful house. His gorgeous wife was upstairs. Their little girl would be here in a few days. And in the near future, a large business deal would be closed with *Worldwide Pathways Incorporated*. Peace was his status and mindset. He smiled to himself as he continued up the stairs.

Damien reached the top steps and walked toward the door of his bedroom. He opened it slowly, trying not to awake his wife. It was still dark in the room and it was obvious that she was still asleep. Julia usually liked to sleep a bit later than he. Especially on a Sunday, he wouldn't expect her up until at least after eight.

As Damien quietly entered the room, he saw his wife sitting up in the bed, holding her stomach. This caught him off guard to see her awake so early, but what really caught his attention was the look on her face. She looked a little worried. Damien spoke softly, "Julia, are you okay?"

Julia shook her head. "No, something's wrong."

Damien stepped closer to her, "What?... What do you mean?"

Julia closed her eyes tightly, "I... I... I don't feel the baby."

"Babe, it's ok," Damien sat beside his wife on the bed, trying to console her. "She's probably just not active right now. It'll be all right."

Julia shook her head. "No, Damien, I can tell something's not right. We need to go the hospital immediately."

Damien couldn't think of what to say or do. A part of him didn't want to believe his wife. All he wanted to do was reassure her that everything was going to be ok. That everything was fine. But he knew in his heart of hearts that there was a real problem. He put his hand on his wife's shoulder to comfort her. "Let me change and we'll leave right away."

ೋ

It had taken Damien and Julia just a few minutes to get ready before leaving for the hospital. Julia already had a small bag packed in anticipation of the birth of their little girl. Damien drove as fast as he could around the beltway toward the hospital where they were planning on delivering. Damien kept twisting his watch out of nervousness as he weaved through the cars on the interstate. Julia was in the passenger side of the Viper, holding her stomach. The tears were streaming down her cheeks. She prayed quietly, "Please God, help her to be ok. You can make her move. You've got the whole world in your hands, surely you can answer this prayer."

They exited off the beltway toward the hospital. Damien felt like he was in a daze. His mind felt blank. As a Marine, he was taught to always think about his next step and how to accomplish the task at hand. The problem at this point was that he couldn't think of what his next step should

41

be. At that moment he longed for the perfect words he could say to comfort his wife.

They pulled into the hospital and quickly found a parking spot not far from the emergency room's entry door. Damien quickly got out of the car and went to the passenger side to help his wife. He held her arm tightly as they walked toward the hospital's entrance. He gently brushed Julia's hair out of her eyes as they approached the door.

The couple entered the emergency room and Damien headed straight for the desk. The room was busy, but thankfully no one was in line. The receptionists noticed Julia was in pain and sprang into action. Pregnant women were seen as a first priority in the emergency room. "Is she having contractions?" one of the receptionists asked.

"I'm... I'm not sure," Damien said, not knowing how to explain the situation. He turned and walked with the receptionist to where his wife was currently standing against a chair, balancing herself. As the receptionist came closer, she could more clearly see the anguish on Julia's face.

"It's our baby," Damien said as they stepped close to Julia. "She seems to be in distress. We need help right away."

"Ok, we'll get you into labor and delivery right away," the receptionist said.

The next few minutes were a whirlwind. The receptionist brought a wheelchair to Julia as a nurse quickly came and wheeled her to the labor and delivery floor of the hospital. Damien was close by her side the whole way. Eventually they entered a quiet hospital room where the nurses helped Julia onto a bed. The nurses performed some initial tests to check on the baby, but they were inconclusive. One of the nurses spoke politely to her, trying to be as reassuring as she could be. "I'm going to call for the ultrasound technician. She should be here shortly."

Julia continued to hold her stomach, hoping and praying for some movement from their little girl. Damien, still not knowing what to do or say, simply ran his fingers through his wife's brown hair. Even though it wasn't long, time seemed to be standing still as they waited for the technician. They wanted answers. Damien was still hoping that his wife was wrong, and everything was truly ok with the baby.

It wasn't much longer until the ultrasound technician came into the room, bringing with her a portable ultrasound machine. She was a young blonde woman who looked fresh out of school, probably in her early twenties. "Hello," she said pleasantly.

"Hi," Damien said quietly.

"Let's get you all situated here," the young woman said. She helped Julia lie down comfortably and got started with preparing her stomach for the ultrasound. The young woman didn't say much as she had been warned that Julia was experiencing some unusual pain. She tried to stay as professional as she could be.

She applied the wand of the machine to Julia's stomach and moved it around. The picture of their baby girl in the womb came on the screen. The young technician stayed focused as she moved the wand from side to side on Julia's stomach. She studied the screen carefully, looking carefully for specific details. Damien squeezed his wife's hand while he looked on the screen. Julia glanced back and forth between the ultrasound technician and the image of their baby. She was hoping that something in the technician's face would give her a clue that baby was fine.

After a minute or two, the technician put down the wand, and looked at the couple with a stunned look on her face. She then spoke quietly, "I'll be right back."

Damien simply nodded in return as the young woman walked out the door. He then turned to his wife. She was squeezing her eyes shut as she lay on the table. Damien rubbed her arm. The room was quiet. Nothing was said. Damien's mind felt empty as they had no idea how to think or feel. It was as if time was inching along for them.

Less than a minute later a female OBGYN doctor came in with the ultrasound technician. "Hello, I'm Dr. Patterson," the woman said politely. She was in her late fifties and had been practicing medicine for many years. She was thin with short grey hair and glasses. "I want to get another look at the ultrasound, if I may."

"Sure," Julia said pulling up her shirt again to show her stomach. The doctor studied the baby on the screen as the technician slowly moved the wand. Damien again reached for his wife's hand and squeezed tightly.

A few minutes passed as the doctor was looking at every image of the baby carefully. Eventually, the doctor spoke out among the silence. "Thank you. That will do." The technician then set the wand down and turned off the machine.

Damien and Julia waited breathlessly in anticipation of what the doctor would say next. They both hoped that the doctor would deliver some good news. She took a deep breath as she closed her eyes and rubbed her forehead. The room was completely silent for a few seconds before the doctor opened her eyes again. She spoke with great sincerity in her voice. "I'm sorry to tell you, but we weren't able to find a heartbeat... your baby has passed away."

Instantly, Damien bent down and hugged his wife as they both wept loudly. The tears flowed as they held each other. Thoughts, dreams, desires they had for their little girl flooded their minds. Julia thought of their home and their little girl's bedroom. She had mental pictures of what it would be like to sing and rock her to sleep at night. Damien's mind went to the tractor he was riding the day before and the thought of giving her rides on it. All of these dreams and desires were all now gone, erased by one simple statement by the doctor.

After a minute Damien released his wife and wiped his eyes. He noticed the young technician wiping her eyes. This was the first time she had ever dealt with this in her young career. Damien addressed the doctor. "Is there any hope? Should we get a second opinion?"

Dr. Patterson shook her head. "I'm sorry... but it does look certain that there isn't a heartbeat." Damien nodded his head as he looked to a side wall. His wife continued to hold tightly to his arm.

The doctor continued, "We're going to give you a few minutes in privacy. I'll be back in soon to check on you, and then we will plan on moving ahead with an induction."

"Ok... thank you," Julia said through her tears.

"You're very welcome. Feel free to call on us if you need anything." The doctor paused for just a moment before walking out the door with the technician. She spoke once more with great compassion in her voice. "And once again... I'm very sorry for your loss."

As the door shut to their hospital room, Damien and Julia both knew that their lives would never be the same. They would now be facing their lives without Lucy. Their dreams were crushed. They felt terribly alone.

The first person Damien and Julia wanted to see was their pastor. His name was Pastor Joseph Thomas. He was a traditional black pastor who had been in ministry for years. Currently he was in his early seventies. He was a compassionate man who was a friend to everyone. His gentle nature was a wonderful gift that was greatly used for his years of service in pastoral ministry.

Pastor Thomas arrived not long after he was called. He knew the Parkers' baby was coming soon, so he was in anticipation of a phone call from them. Currently, he sat in a chair beside Julia, speaking compassionately to her. "Honey, I'm so sorry this happened to you."

"Thank you," Julia said through her tears. At this point she sat in a hospital bed reclining against a few pillows.

"Never forget, that you and your little girl are precious to the Lord. This grieves him even more than it grieves us."

Damien was on the other side of his bed gently rubbing his wife's arm. He nodded politely in response to his pastor's comment.

Pastor Thomas continued, "Now, before I go, I want to read you both a psalm. And I know it may not seem true right now, but know that at this moment it is truer than it ever has been."

The pastor opened his well-worn Bible to a familiar passage of Scripture, Psalm 23, and began reading with great dignity in his voice. "'The LORD is my shepherd, I shall not want. He maketh me to lie down in green pastures. He leadeth me beside the still waters. He restoreth my soul: He leadeth me in the paths of righteousness for his name's sake.'"

Damien looked away for a moment. A part of him didn't want to hear this right now. His little girl had just passed. He didn't want to hear how the Lord was with them. It didn't feel truthful. *Couldn't God have stopped what just happened?* he thought to himself. *And besides that, where was God leading them now?* They felt alone, and without hope. *God isn't here*, Damien thought to himself.

Pastor Thomas continued, "'Yea, though I walk through the valley of the shadow of death, I will fear no evil: for thou art with me; thy rod and thy staff they comfort me. Thou preparest a table before me in the presence of mine enemies: thou anointest my head with oil; my cup runneth over. Surely goodness and mercy shall follow me all the days of my life: and I will dwell in the house of the LORD forever.'"

Pastor Thomas closed his Bible and smiled at the couple. He knew they both had a long history with the church and the Bible and that no further explanation would be needed. He continued, "I'm going to leave you two, but do feel free to call on me anytime. I love you, guys, and know that you will be in our thoughts and prayers."

"Thank you so much, Pastor," Julia said with a slight smile.

"Bless you, child," Pastor Thomas said as he bent down and gave her a small kiss on the forehead. He then looked up at Damien on the other side of the bed. He held out his hand. "I'll be praying for you too, Damien. Don't forget to cry out for help if you need it."

Damien reached out and shook his pastor's hand, gripping it tightly. "I will. Thanks for coming."

"Love you," the pastor said one last time before turning and leaving the room. Julia wiped the tears away from her eyes as she continued to cry.

Looking at his wife, Damien tried to think of something he could do in this moment. He paced the room, not knowing how he should feel or think. "I'm going to head to the bathroom," he said to his wife.

"Wait!" she said, calling out to him. She reached out her arms for an embrace from him. He walked over and threw his arms around her one more time. They held each other close. Julia spoke softly into her husband's ear, "I love you, Damien."

"I love you too," Damien answered. He gave his wife one more tight squeeze before heading into the small bathroom in their room.

Many friends and family came by throughout the day as they were in the hospital waiting for their baby girl to be born. Most of their church family had called, texted, or stopped by when they heard the news. Even though friends and family didn't know what to say, it meant a lot to Julia especially that they came. People would just come by and express their concern and care, often not saying anything more than, "We love you, and we're praying for you."

Damien, on the other hand, was struggling. He wanted to comfort his wife but felt emotionally drained himself. He had faced a lot of obstacles and challenges during his time in the Marines, but this overshadowed all of them. He felt helpless. He felt weak, and he didn't know what to do. Damien always took his role of a husband seriously, but at this moment he didn't know how to be strong and a good support for his loving wife.

The day progressed slowly. Damien fell in and out of sleep. It wasn't until just after midnight that one of the nurses woke him up to tell him his wife was going into labor. He went and stood beside her, still in the hospital bed. Julia wasn't in much pain as she had received an epidural. The doctors and nurses all quickly got into their proper place as the Parkers awaited instruction. All the medical professionals were sensitive and exceptionally caring during the whole process.

The labor went smoothly, and after fifteen minutes, Damien and Julia saw their little girl, Lucy. She did not make a sound. She did not open her eyes. But she was beautiful. She measured just under seven pounds and twenty inches long. With the nurses' help, the doctor then cut the umbilical cord and handed little Lucy to her mother.

Julia was crying heavily at this point. The tears were a mixture of both joy and sadness. Even though there was no life in the body of her child, she loved her greatly. This was her daughter. She would always be her firstborn. She would never be forgotten. Julia gently ran her fingers through Lucy's soft black hair. Damien watched from the side of the hospital bed. He fought back tears as hard as he could as he admired his young daughter. He picked up one of her little hands and lifted her fingers. They looked so perfect, so well formed. She was a miracle. She was his little girl.

Damien and Julia held their girl through the night as they knew this was the only time in this life they would get to spend with her. They held onto every memory, as they didn't want this night to ever end. Many pictures were taken, and eventually in the early morning hours of the next day they handed their little Lucy to one of the nurses that had been with them since the beginning. They would never forget that moment of the nurse leaving the room with their little girl in her arms. Life would never be the same.

Chapter 4

Monday was a difficult day for the Parkers. They were still in the hospital as Julia was recovering from the delivery. Damien and Julia tried to sleep as much as they could. Friends continued to come by, offering their love and support. Julia's father and mother had arrived the night before and visited off and on throughout the day. Julia was thankful to have them close by.

Damien was still struggling with the whole process. He didn't know how to think or feel. At times he felt faint. In the middle of the afternoon, Julia awoke to find him in a chair beside her rubbing his forehead. He didn't look well. "Damien, are you ok?" Julia asked concerned.

"Yeah, I'll be fine," he said softly. He was sweating just a little.

"Have you eaten anything today?"

Damien shook his head. In everything that had occurred, he had simply forgotten to eat.

Julia reached over and put her hand on his shoulder. Damien looked over to see the concern in his wife's eyes. "Honey, you need to take care of yourself."

Damien looked down at the ground as he continued to rub his forehead. "I know…" the words were coming with great difficulty for him. "I just… haven't been hungry, that's all."

Damien and Julia sat in silence for a few moments before Julia spoke up again. "Ok… Damien, why don't you go to the cafeteria and get something. You need to try to eat."

"But… I don't want to leave you here by yourself. What if…" his voice trailed off as he searched for the right words.

His wife responded as compassionately as she could. "I'll be fine. I want you to take care of yourself for right now. It'll be good for you."

Damien nodded briefly as he knew his wife was right. He stood to his feet. "Ok, I'm going to… use the restroom, and then I'll go down."

Julia smiled in return. "Ok, I love you."

"Love you too," Damien said faintly.

Damien went into the bathroom and shut the door behind him. He shuffled toward the sink and turned it on full strength. He put his hands on the side of the sink as he bent over it. He then took a deep breath before looking at himself directly in the mirror. It had been a long day and a half. He had been up and down emotionally, thinking about how he could best comfort his wife. Damien felt hopeless. He felt abandoned. He had no idea as to what his next move should be.

Through it all, he began to fill one emotion beginning to well up inside of him—anger. *Why did this happen to him? Why did this happen to his wife?* She was ready for a child to pour out her love to. *Why did Lucy have to die? This was unfair. This should have never happened to her.* His life felt broken. His faith felt shaken.

He started to walk away, but the anger was too strong. He couldn't contain it. In one quick moment Damien lifted his arm and with the back of his hand hit the mirror that was over the sink. It severely cracked where his hand made contact. A few shards of glass came off with his knuckles as he pulled away from the mirror. Damien looked down at his fist to see that it was bleeding a little from the impact. He quickly put his hand under the faucet to wash away the blood.

"You fool, Damien," he whispered to himself as he washed his hand. As the water ran over his hand, he noticed something strange. He turned off the water to get a closer look. He examined it closely and he could see a tiny crack on the face of his watch. Looking even closer he noticed something even more peculiar. His watch had stopped working. He shook it to see if it would start up again. It was in vain.

Damien cussed under his breath. Now he had also broken his watch.

❦

A few days after the Parkers left the hospital, they had a funeral for their little girl. The service was well attended. Along with their church family, longtime friends came from far and near to attend the service. Lots of flowers were sent along with many monetary gifts. The Parkers had requested that all financial contributions be directed to the Wounded Warriors Foundation, supporting those who had been injured while serving on active duty. The gifts totaled a few thousand dollars. All the loved poured out on the Parkers helped Julia to feel a glimmer of hope through it all.

The graveside service for Lucy, attended by family only, was a more emotional time. Pastor Thomas delivered a message about comfort and the love of God. He read various passages throughout the whole Bible. It was a message that balanced both grief and hope evenly. Many tears were shed as family members laid flowers on top of Lucy's small casket. Through the service Damien sat with his head down, contemplating the whole event. Currently he didn't want to hear it. Messages of hope were not what he was ready for. He wanted answers. He wanted to know why. He wanted to ask Pastor Thomas, *"Where was God when my little girl died? Why was God not there?"*

The service ended with one final prayer, and Damien abruptly got up to leave. His wife grabbed his arm. She knew her husband well enough to know he was struggling with everything. They made eye contact as he looked down at her. She spoke through her tears, "Will you stay with me? Just for a moment."

Damien took a deep breath and quietly sat down beside her. Clouds covered the sky. Rain had been predicted later, but at the moment everything was calm. Family began to stand to their feet and very quietly mingle. Like many funerals, it brought family members together who hadn't seen one another for quite some time. Both sides of the family were well represented.

Damien's dad walked up and put his hand on his son's shoulder. Damien looked up and saw a compassionate expression on his father's face. His father was never a man of much emotion, but at this point Damien could see the tears in his eyes as he spoke. "Son, I just want to let you know I'm here if you need me."

"Thank you," Damien said softly. His dad simply patted him on the shoulder as he slowly walked away.

Damien turned back to see his wife with tears streaming down her face as she sat staring at the casket. She squeezed her husband's hand as she wiped her eyes. Damien wanted to say something to help, something that could bring healing. But hopelessness overshadowed him. *Where was this hope Pastor Thomas was just talking about?* He thought to himself. Maybe there was no hope. Maybe this would be the new normal. Maybe this is what life would now be like living in light of his daughter's death.

He couldn't take any more of this. Damien stood to his feet. "I got to go," he said abruptly to his wife.

Julia was caught off guard, but could tell her husband was struggling. "Ok," she replied.

Damien said nothing else as he turned and headed back to their car. He didn't want to speak with any family at this time. Julia watched him as he walked away. She was worried about him. She said a little prayer, "God, please help him. He needs you now."

As he was about to open the door to his car, Damien was stopped by someone placing a hand on his shoulder. "Damien."

Damien turned to see his senior business partner Henry Wheaton behind him. Being as close as he was to Damien and Julia, he was the one person at the graveside who wasn't family. "Hey," Damien said, almost emotionless. Because Henry was much older, Damien tried to portray himself as strong around him. In a sense it was as if subconsciously he felt he needed to further prove that he was a worthy partner to such a successful businessman. Even though Henry often saw right through it, Damien tried not to show signs of weakness.

"Listen, I just want you know I'm praying for you," Henry spoke with great sincerity in his voice. "And feel free to take all the time you need in coming back to work. There's no rush, my friend." Damien simply nodded his head as he bit his lip. He was ready to be alone.

"You take care of yourself, ok?" Henry said, patting his partner on the side of his arm.

"Thanks, Henry," Damien said as he opened the door to the car. "We'll be in touch." As Henry walked away, Damien slid himself into the driver's seat of his vehicle and shut the door.

Henry couldn't help but turn and take one last look before walking away. He wished there was something else he could've said to him. He thought a lot of Damien and truly would do anything he could to help him heal from this loss. After losing his wife years ago, he had become more closed off to others. Damien's partnership and friendship were a key factor in helping him return to his old self. He wanted to help Damien in the same way he had helped him. *What else could I have done to help him? Is there something else I could've said?* Henry thought to himself. He wiped a tear from his eye as he continued to walk away.

Damien took a deep breath as he leaned his head against the back of his seat. He loosened his tie, trying to get comfortable. He was glad the service was over. This pain of losing his child was too much for him to bear. He was ready to move forward and get on with life.

As if on instinct he looked at the time on his watch, forgetting that it had stopped working a few days ago. Damien sighed in frustration. He was still wearing it out of habit. In the next couple of days, he hoped to take it into a shop and get it worked on. As he looked at the watch again, he noticed that the crack in the glass had gotten a little bigger. He rubbed his fingers over the face, hoping it was a smudge. To his disappointment he found that the crack had indeed grown. "Great," he said sarcastically. Damien just shook his head in frustration as he sat staring at his watch. Life was dealing him a rotten hand. First, he had lost his mother when he was much too young, and now his first daughter with the same name had been taken from him. In the past his thoughts and emotions about the loss of his mom were something he suppressed and tried not to dwell on. Also, this watch had helped serve as a reminder of her love for him... but now even that was busted. On top of everything he already carried in life, he had no idea how he'd carry this pain of the loss of his daughter. It seemed impossible. It seemed hopeless.

Chapter 5

Time continued to move slowly. About three weeks had passed since Lucy was born. Friends and family stopped by daily. They brought with them meals, flowers, and cards. Julia continued to feel loved and supported through it all. Oftentimes she would just sit and cry with a friend. No one ever seemed to have the right words to say, but that was fine. She felt their compassion. She felt their love. Their church family was a wonderful support, going above and beyond, helping wherever they could. Pastor Thomas would call or stop by every few days and lend his love and support. He truly had a gift of empathy and compassion.

Besides simply taking a few calls, Damien hadn't been back to work yet. The deal with *Worldwide Pathways Incorporated* was still in the works. The planned trip to Nevis was only two days away. Damien had the trip in mind for the time he would start back at work full-time. He looked forward to it as he was still struggling emotionally and thought his work schedule would help him heal.

Currently Julia was sitting on the couch in their living room, looking through a box of old pictures. She was dressed comfortably and had the pictures spread out on the couch. Her body was still recovering, and she had been experiencing some pain as of late. The last few days she had been trying to take it easy and not exert too much energy. She found simple tasks like this to be exactly what she needed.

She heard the door shut as Damien walked in the house. He had been out for a jog. He entered the living room and was surprised to see Julia looking through the pictures. "What are you doing?"

She smiled slightly as she spoke. "I'm just looking through these old photos."

Damien stepped forward to get a closer look at the pictures. He could see they were their old baby pictures. "Why are you looking at those?"

Julia looked up. She was still smiling. "I wanted to see who Lucy looked like. I wondered if she favored you or me."

Damien sat on the edge of the couch and shook his head. "Are you sure you should be doing this?"

"Why not?" Julia said as her gaze was once again fixed on the pictures.

He shrugged his shoulders. "I don't know. I mean..." He rubbed his hand over his head as he searched for the words to say. "Do you think this is good for you?"

"Absolutely. She was our little girl. It's something I want to do right now." Julia held a picture over to where her husband could see it. "Look at this one of you. I think she had your nose, and maybe…"

Damien stood to his feet, interrupting his wife. "No, Julia, I don't think I'm ready for this."

Julia was caught off guard a little. "Ok, it's no problem. You don't have to look at anything."

"I'm sorry. I…" Damien searched for the words to say, but they didn't come to him. He greatly desired to be a comfort and support to his wife, but he knew that at the moment he couldn't look at these pictures. "I'm just going to get some water."

"Ok, take your time," Julia said sincerely.

Damien entered the kitchen and grabbed a glass out of the cupboard. He had just run six miles. Jogging helped to get his mind off the sorrow that was in his life. He drank his water quickly and set his glass down. He looked out the window that was over the sink. The grass was starting to grow longer. Damien thought back to the day before Lucy was born. It was such a peaceful day and he didn't have a care in the world, just excitement and anticipation of the day of her birth. He wished he could go back to that day.

He abruptly turned aside from the window. He didn't want to dwell on the past any longer. He was done with looking backward. The trip to Nevis was two days away and he needed to start planning for it. It had the potential to be the biggest account *Parker & Wheaton Marketing* had ever seen. That was where his focus needed to be; not on the past, not on his daughter.

Damien went back to the living room and found his wife leaning back on the couch and rubbing her stomach. "Are you all right?"

Her eyes squeezed tight like she was in pain. "I'm not sure."

Damien went and sat beside his wife. "Is it that same stomach pain that's been bothering you?"

"Yeah, but it's worse. I don't know what's going on." Julia had been experiencing some pain ever since her labor. At first, she thought it was normal pain for someone recovering from giving birth, but in the last few days it had been getting more severe.

"Is there something I can get for you?"

Julia struggled to speak. "Maybe just a glass of water."

"Ok," Damien said, standing to his feet. He quickly headed to the kitchen but was stopped by Julia before he entered.

"Damien!"

"Yes?"

She took a deep breath. "On second thought, I think we need to go to the hospital."

"Ok. Let me help you out to the car," he said urgently.

Damien and Julia went right to the hospital's emergency room. They waited for about fifteen minutes before being admitted. Julia was seen by a few nurses before the doctor came in to see her. He checked several things on her and did a few x-rays. The wait for results seemed like an excruciating long time for Damien and Julia as they sat alone in a hospital room. Eventually it was determined that Julia was suffering from a small amount of internal bleeding and would require a minor surgery soon. Thankfully the doctor was able to schedule it for early the following day. Julia would need to be kept overnight to monitor her status as she was in a large amount of pain. The one comfort for them was that the surgery would happen the next morning and they wouldn't have to wait long.

It was close to noon the following day when Julia awoke from surgery. Everything had gone well. The problem was in her lower stomach, where in an irregular incidence, Julia had suffered a small tear. The doctors were able to go in and do a simple repair to fix the tear. Julia would have a few days of recovering in the hospital, but overall, she was just thankful this problem had been dealt with.

Julia's mother and Damien were by her side. Damien was the first face she saw as she opened her eyes. "Hey, how are you feeling?" he said to her.

"I'm ok," Julia said, tired.

"The doctors said the surgery went well and they think they were able to repair everything properly."

Julia closed her eyes and smiled a little. "Great to hear." She then turned her attention to her mother. "Hi, Mom."

"Hello, Sweetheart," she stood close to Julia and grabbed her hand. "I came as soon as I heard. You've been through so much lately. I didn't want you guys to have to bear this alone."

"Thanks," Julia said. Damien nodded in agreement.

It wasn't much longer until the doctor came in. He was in his early fifties, wore glasses, and was hearing a white coat over a dress shirt and tie. He was the epitome of a professional. "Hello," he announced as he entered the room. He had two x-rays in his right hand. He showed the x-rays to Julia and Damien and explained to them the extent of the surgery and what had occurred. Apparently, Julia had a small internal tear from the pregnancy that had failed to heal on its own. Over the last three weeks the tear seemed to get worse through the normal day-to-day activities, thus increasing in pain as time had passed.

Damien was the first to speak after the doctor's report. "Is everything fine now? When can she go home?"

The doctor briefly shrugged his shoulders before speaking up. "I think it might be best if we hold her overnight. Just to watch and be sure the repair doesn't open back up. We are probably looking at an afternoon discharge." The doctor then offered a little more information before leaving.

The room was silent for just a few moments before Damien spoke up, "It sounds like good news from the doctor."

"I agree," Julia's mother added. Julia gave a tired half-smile as she took in the news.

"Do you need anything?" Damien asked.

"No, I really do feel fine. Maybe just a little sore, but overall not much pain," Julia said. Her head was resting comfortably on a pillow.

Julia's mother walked over to her bedside and gently rubbed her daughter's arm. More than anything she wished she could have borne some of these trials her daughter had faced. She spoke with deep compassion in her voice, "You two have had quite a rocky road this last month."

"Yeah," Julia responded. She reached up and grabbed her mother's hand.

The three sat comfortably together through the afternoon. They didn't talk about much as the last three weeks had been filled with so much sorrow. The afternoon flowed into the evening, and they simply waited in the hospital room. Eventually Julia turned on the television and watched reruns on the Food Network. A couple of nurses had come in periodically to check on her, but overall everything was quiet.

As the evening continued on, Damien kept thinking about his impending trip to Nevis the next day. He had talked with Julia's mother about it earlier. She thought it should be fine, since she was going to stay with her daughter and could take her home. Damien hadn't brought up the conversation yet with Julia. He wasn't sure how she would respond, but he figured he ought to approach the topic before it got much later in the evening.

"Julia," he said with great timidity in his voice. She turned her head to face him. It was as if she knew what he was about to say. He continued, "I think I might need to get going. As you know, I have to leave for St. Kitts and Nevis early tomorrow."

"Damien..." she looked at him very sincerely. "Are you sure this is a good idea?"

Damien stood to his feet and spoke quietly. "Yes... I know it's not the best timing for any of us. But I think I better go, being this is one of our company's biggest deals ever."

Julia closed her eyes and took a deep breath before speaking. "I really don't think you should go. It is..."

"I understand," he said, gently interrupting her. "I know you just went through surgery, but your mother said she would stay and help you. I think you will be fine."

"No!" Julia said urgently. She reached over and grabbed her husband's hand. "It's not me I'm worried about."

"What do you mean?"

"It's not me... it's you, Damien."

The words struck him hard. "What?"

She pulled him closer, continuing to speak sincerely. "You're still dealing with the loss of Lucy. I know you try to hide it, but I see it in you. You're struggling. I don't think it's a good time for you to be gone. It's like a shadow is lying over you, Damien."

"Julia..." Damien said, trying to redirect the conversation. "I'm fine. Yes, we've been through a lot, but the best medicine for me is to keep going. We don't have..."

"Please... listen to what I'm saying. You can't keep it buried. It's going to grow, come out periodically, and in the end make you bitter."

Damien turned to the side and shook his head. He didn't want to keep thinking about this right now. The trip to Nevis and the deal with *Worldwide Pathways* was tomorrow. And though he and his wife had dealt with a lot recently, this deal had the potential to be a game changer for them. If the death of his daughter was a low valley in their lives, this deal could be a mountaintop. And Damien was ready to make that journey. "I'm sorry, Julia… I have to go. This isn't just some ordinary deal for *Parker & Wheaton Marketing.* It's a game changer. You'll understand when I get back why I had to go. You'll be fine. Trust me."

Julia couldn't hold her frustration in any longer. "Stop worrying about me!" She took another deep breath, and tightly squeezed his hand. "You need to start taking care of yourself."

Damien looked off to the side and bit his lip. He was ready for this conversation to end. His mind needed to be on business. It needed to be on the task at hand. He couldn't afford to journey back into some of the hurt of the last few weeks. Not now, maybe not ever. He didn't know what to say. He simply bent down and kissed his wife on the forehead. A few words stuttered out of his mouth. "Look…I'll… I can call you before I get on the plane tomorrow. I should be back the following day."

A tear rolled down Julia's cheek as he turned and walked to the door. "Goodbye, and thank you," he said to his mother-in-law before opening the door. She simply waved and mouthed the words "you're welcome" in return.

As Damien was about to walk out, Julia called out. "Damien!"

"Yes?"

She looked right into his eyes as she spoke with great sincerity. "I'll be praying for you. I love you."

He nodded his head before speaking. "Thanks, I love you too," he said quietly as he turned to walk away.

Damien Parker went home and started packing his bags. The bedroom television was on. He was trying to distract himself as he wasn't in a good state emotionally. The last three weeks had been an emotional roller coaster for him, and Julia's present state was another twist in their lives. He truly loved her and wished he could be there with her. At any other time, there would be no question that he was going to stay with her.

Since the passing of Lucy three weeks ago, their marriage had been strained. They weren't communicating well with one another and much of the laughter of their home had left. Damien knew that this was mostly his fault. He had closed himself off. It wasn't a conscious decision. It was just indicative of his personality. When pain arose in his life, he worked hard at suppressing his emotions, striving to stay strong and poised. The difficult thing in this current situation was that he didn't know the approach to take. He didn't know how to move forward.

He sat on the edge of his bed as the television continued with the late local news. He grew tired of it. Grabbing the remote, Damien turned it off and laid back on the bed. He took a deep breath as he stared up at the ceiling. He knew that the trip ahead needed his full focus and attention. Nothing could get in the way. This was going to be the deal of a lifetime.

With greater resolve, Damien stood to his feet and continued with the packing. There was a job at hand. Tomorrow, he would leave for St. Kitts and Nevis and get the deal done.

෨ඉ

Julia couldn't sleep. The lights were off in the hospital room. Her mom was beside her sleeping soundly in a recliner. They hadn't said much to one another since Damien left. Julia's mind was preoccupied with her husband. As she had said earlier in the evening, she was worried about him. And particularly, she was worried about this trip. She wasn't sure what it was exactly, but she knew he needed help.

As a person of strong faith, she did what she always did when she was worried. She prayed. "God, please be with Damien. He needs you now more than ever. I'm so worried for him." She paused a moment as tears started to flow. She wasn't sure what exactly to pray but thought it best just to place the whole situation in God's hands. "Somehow, help him to heal. Show him that he needs you... that he needs others. This is not something he can bear on his own. Intervene in his life. Get his attention. Show him that he needs to deal with this trial and not bury it." Julia paused a moment as she felt her resolve begin to grow stronger. "And I know that whatever he faces, you will work it together for good in his life. Please be near him in a special way... and I

69

pray these things in your name, God, and the name of your son, the Lord Jesus. Amen."

Julia took a deep breath and closed her eyes. She knew that it was now out of her hands. Fifteen minutes later, she was sound asleep.

Chapter 6

Damien entered the Raleigh-Durham airport, dressed professionally in a suit and tie. His carry-on was over his shoulder. It was just after 6:00am. He arrived about an hour and fifteen minutes before his flight departed. Having departed from this airport numerous times, he knew that he had plenty of time to get through security and to his departure gate. The plan was for him to meet up with his partner, Henry, and the lawyer, Rufus, at the terminal. Knowing Henry, he'd probably been there for fifteen minutes already.

Going through security, he removed his shoes like always and emptied his pockets. He was greeted by the TSA agent. "Good morning, Mr. Parker." The airport wasn't very busy this morning.

"Hello, Frank," he said nonchalantly.

"Where you headed this time?" the agent said without breaking his focus.

"The island of Nevis, not far from St. Kitts."

"Hmm… sounds nice," he said as he motioned for Damien to walk through the metal detector.

The alarm went off, surprising both the agent and Damien. He knew he had removed his belt and the items out of his pockets. The agent quickly looked Damien over and simply mentioned, "Your watch."

Damien looked down and saw his watch still on his wrist. He chuckled to himself as he forgot he was still wearing it. In the late night of packing, he hadn't taken it off when he went to bed. "Sorry about that," he said. He slid it off and put it in a plastic bowl to go through the conveyer belt. He then walked through the metal detector again and this time everything was fine. He grabbed his watch and put it back on his wrist. A passing thought came through Damien's mind just to take it and throw it in the trash. It was still not working and the crack in it reminded him of breaking it in the hospital after Lucy was born. Those were memories he didn't want to keep reliving.

Arriving at the terminal, he found Henry patiently waiting for him. He was also dressed in a suit. He stood to his feet as Damien approached. Like Damien, he was tall, 6'3". He had played wide receiver at a small college in his younger years. Since then he prided himself on staying fit and exercising regularly. The two men shook hands as they met. "Damien, good to see you."

"You too," Damien responded. The two hadn't seen much of each other since the funeral. Damien had only been in the office a few days, and most of those days Henry was gone to the northeastern part of the country.

"Sorry about Julia. I'm glad to hear the surgery went well," Henry said. Damien had been texting him updates over the last couple of days.

"Yeah, her mom's staying with her now. The doctors said she should be discharged later today."

Henry rubbed his chin as he listened to Damien's words. He knew his partner had been through a lot recently and Henry wanted him to know that he cared for him as a friend as well as a business partner. "Look, Damien." He put his hand on his partner's shoulder. "If you really think you should be with her now, then I definitely understand. Please, don't feel like you have to be here for me. This deal can..."

He wasn't able to finish as Damien interrupted him. "Henry, please, we're fine. She's fine. It's time we get back to work."

Henry shrugged his shoulders. He spoke sincerely, "Ok... I just know you guys have had some huge trials these past few weeks, and I want to be sure you've taken the time you need to heal. It won't bother me at all if you need more time away."

Damien rolled his eyes. He was starting to get frustrated. This was starting to sound very similar to the speech Julia had given him before he left the hospital. He didn't want to hear it again from Henry. "No, we aren't talking about this now. We're about to make the biggest deal of our career. That's where our focus needs to be. I don't want to hear you say another thing about my family. You got that?"

Henry didn't know how to respond. He'd never seen this type of emotion from his partner before. It was a tense scene as the two men just stood staring back at one another. It was then that Damien saw from the corner of his eye Rufus walking toward them. "Here's Rufus," he said quietly. He had recognized him right away. Rufus was 5'7" in stature with brown hair and glasses.

Henry turned to see Rufus coming close. "Hey, fellows." Rufus sounded upbeat.

"Hello, Rufus," Damien said, extending his hand for a shake.

"You guys ready to see the Caribbean?" he said with a little bit of a laughter in his voice. Rufus Donaldson was twenty-nine years old, but at times acted like he was still in college. He'd never been married and never seemed to keep a girlfriend more than a month or two. He partied hard and drank on the weekends. Damien had hired him two years prior. His credentials were exceptional, and his education honors were top-notch. It wasn't until three months into his job that Damien and Henry started noticing his terrible personal habits. They were an item of concern to them both, but one thing they couldn't argue with was Rufus' work. He was exceptional in his skill as a lawyer, particularly in inspecting contracts. He could quickly spot flaws that would need to be reworded or restructured. He also had a strange hobby of following tax law. This also proved to be valuable on occasion. Overall Rufus was an outstanding lawyer.

"Yeah, well, remember this meeting comes first," Henry reminded him. "I'm not sure how long it's going to take, but you keep your mind sharp in our meeting."

Rufus laughed. "I hear you. But, hey, as soon as we're free, I'm hitting the beach with a margarita in hand." Damien turned to look away. It was times like this that he had to remind himself that Rufus was a good lawyer, and not just some irresponsible frat boy. Though sometimes Damien wondered if his skill as a lawyer was worth putting up with all this mischief.

The door opened to their flight's jetway, and an overhead voice called for their flight. A big smile came over Rufus' face. "Well, shall we?"

"Most definitely," Damien said as the three began walking toward the boarding pass scanner. A line was already forming before they could get there. Though it didn't look like the flight would be full, it did appear to have a substantial number of passengers.

As they approached the jetway Henry grabbed ahold of Damien's arm. He turned to face his partner. "Look, Damien," Henry said quietly. He wanted to finish with their conversation from earlier. "If on this trip, you need to take a moment or two, or if you need to talk, I definitely understand. I'm here for you."

Damien simply nodded his head as he turned back toward the plane's entrance. He didn't want to hear anything else about his family's difficult times. He wanted to shut it all off until he arrived back. His mind was on the deal with *Worldwide Pathways.* He wanted this deal. He needed this deal.

༶ঌয়঺

After a two-hour layover in Puerto Rico, the three men arrived on the island of St. Kitts in the middle of the afternoon. The plan was for them to take a ferry to the smaller island of Nevis, just under two miles from St. Kitts. The flights had been smooth, and the layover was seamless. Damien faked sleeping during the trip as he wasn't in the mood for talking. Henry spent his time solving Sudoku puzzles and reading a book on his phone. Rufus, on the other hand, listened to music on his headphones. Nevertheless, when they arrived on the island, all three men put aside their flight habits and sprung into a business mindset.

It was a beautiful day in St. Kitts. The skies were clear, and the sun was shining bright. The island was beautiful. One could easily see the rich vegetation and rolling landscape. The airport itself was surrounded by large hills that gave the area even more of a look of beauty. The island was only eighteen miles long at its maximum length. Together with the smaller island of Nevis, they formed a nation. The residents of the island weren't rich, but there was enough wealth brought in from tourism to give most residents a quality standard of living. Riding in a taxi on their way to the ferry, Damien took notice of the residents. They looked to be peaceful people who seemed content with their lives. They were of African descent and shared accents closely with those of Jamaica.

Earlier the men had briefly stopped by their hotel and dropped off their bags. Their hotel was one of the closest to the airport. When Damien went to book the hotel, he debated with himself whether it would be advantageous to stay on St. Kitts or Nevis. In the end he thought it would be best to stay close to the airport just in case there was a problem with the ferries on the day they would plan to leave. They would just have to be sure to catch a late ferry back across to St. Kitts before the end of the day. The other possibility was to see if *Worldwide Pathways* had a private boat that could transport them. It was all simply a minor nuisance they would need to keep in mind.

Currently, the three men were on the ferry traveling to the smaller island of Nevis. They tried to relax as it was a 45-minute ride from their port on St. Kitts to the Nevis port. All three of the men had their coats off and their ties were loosened. Rufus was currently making small talk with a couple of college students who were retelling some of the stories of fun they had while on the island. Henry and Damien were talking casually, while leaning on one of the boat's railings, looking out onto the ocean. They were going over some of the details that would need to be discussed in this meeting.

"Have you heard from Julia today?" Henry asked, changing the conversation.

"Yes, she's feeling well. They discharged her from the hospital earlier in the day. No problems. She was ready to be home."

"Good to hear," Henry said, looking out onto the ocean water as the ferry moved along. "How was her hospital experience?"

"The doctors and nurses were great," Damien said, looking over at Henry. "I'd recommend the place to anyone. The rooms are nice, and the staff took good care of her."

"Well, I'm happy to hear that. I remember one time my wife had a simple procedure there, but it was outpatient. Nothing like what you guys have been through." Damien simply nodded in return. The last statement by Henry quieted the conversation. Damien was ready to change the topic of conversation.

They stood in silence for a few moments, taking in the beautiful scenery of the Caribbean. Henry was anxious to keep the conversation going as things had been a little tense earlier in the day. He figured he would shift the conversation back to the meeting that would take place soon.

"Who exactly is going to be in this meeting?" Henry asked.

"From what I gather, the CEO, the shipping manager for the southern Florida region, along with a lawyer," Damien responded.

"Hmm... that's an interesting group. I wonder why the majority owner isn't going to be there."

"Not sure," Damien said. "I figured these were the guys in the company who would know for sure if we could suit their needs and bring in the type of clients they're looking for. If these guys are persuaded, then it should be no problem convincing the owners that we are the company they need. It should be a slam dunk."

"Huh." From the beginning Henry had questions about this meeting and though he wasn't totally sure what it was, his intuition told him that something wasn't adding up. "I wonder..." he said, thinking out loud. "Why did they want to meet here on the island? If this shipping manager works out of Florida, why didn't we just meet there?"

"I don't know, but I wouldn't think too much of it. I just figured the CEO or the company must have a place down here."

The ferry continued to move along, slicing through the water. They were now close to the island of Nevis. It was at that time that Rufus joined them. "Damien, too bad you couldn't get us a place here on Nevis. Some of those guys were telling me about some of the beaches and what's cool to see over here."

Damien shook his head. "Rufus, you worry about the beaches later. You help us land this deal, and I'll probably join you." Damien smiled briefly as he turned to Henry. "And, hey, I'll even drag Henry out there with us."

Henry chuckled slightly. "Now that is one place you will never find me. I know I'm from North Carolina, but between the sand and the heat, I am not a fan of the beach."

"Oh, we'll find a way to get you there," Rufus said jovially. "You'll be riding the waves with me in no time."

"Don't count on it."

The meeting was to take place at a hotel on the coast. The hotel was exquisite, consisting of five-star amenities and beachfront views. Most would describe it as a "paradise" resort. Arriving at the resort via taxi, the three men noticed that the place looked relatively vacant. Three black SUVs were in the parking lot with a man in a suit waiting by them. He was clearly an associate of the company. The taxi pulled up close to the building and the three men exited the cab.

"Welcome to Nevis," the associate said.

"Thank you," Henry responded.

"Right this way," the associate said as he led the way up the steps and through the glass doors of the resort. Once again, Henry and Damien noticed how empty the place was. No one else was in sight, and in particular, not even any employees for the resort. Henry thought this was bizarre, to say the least. It was summertime and he expected at least a few residents to be staying there. They walked past a window and Henry looked out onto the patio and the beach. There were no residents out on the patio either. That confirmed it in his mind that the place was completely empty.

The men were led to an outdoor meeting area with a canopy overhead and enclosed by a stone wall. A beautiful stone walkway led the way and marked off the area. There was a long wooden table that looked as if it would seat sixteen guests. Chairs were set up around it. Fans were running to keep the area cool. The meeting area felt professional but relaxed. The sun was still shining since it was 4:00 in the afternoon. It was a beautiful day.

But none of the décor mattered to the three men. They were stunned as they entered the area. Before them stood a gathering of a dozen men, all dressed in suits. All stood with their gaze fixed on Henry, Damien, and Rufus. To say it was intimating would be an understatement.

"Greetings," said the man who stood in the middle of the group. He appeared to be in his mid-seventies with grey hair. He was thin and over six feet in height. A white beard covered the bottom half of his face. In one hand he was holding a cane. He was dressed professionally in a three-piece suit.

"Thanks for having us," Henry said, somewhat stoic.

The grey-haired man held out his hand. "My name is Lex Williamson. I'm the majority owner of *Worldwide Pathways*." His voice was raspy and very distinct.

Damien and Rufus also shook hands with Mr. Williamson. "The pleasure is mine," Damien said as he introduced himself. "Damien Parker." Many other introductions were made around the room. There were too many men for Damien, Henry, and Rufus to remember all the names and titles. It was three minutes later that everyone sat down, and the meeting began.

Mr. Williamson began, "Once again, thank you for meeting with us today." Three files filled with documents were passed out to Damien, Henry, and Rufus.

Henry didn't know what to say as the size of the group was not what he expected. "You're welcome," Henry forced himself to say.

"From our earlier talks and exploration of your company, we feel a partnership with you might be what we are looking for." Mr. Williamson was calm as he relayed the information.

Damien spoke up. "Yes sir, the last two years have been highly successful for us. The companies we've worked with have reported successful results from using our services."

Mr. Williamson smiled, "Good... that's great to hear."

The next hour was filled with lots of questions from the associates of *Worldwide Pathways*. Most of the questions were specific financial questions that had to do with the success *Parker & Wheaton* had with other companies they worked with. Some of them were very technical. Damien answered most of the questions. He tried to project confidence as best as he could. Rufus was listening intently while also scanning the documents presented to him. Occasionally, he would take notes on what he was hearing or reading.

Throughout the meeting, Mr. Williamson sat back in his chair, relaxed. After one of Damien's success stories about the company, he spoke up, showing his pleasure. "Yes, researching your company, honestly, I feel confident that you can find us the specific clientele we're looking for."

Damien was also smiling at this point. "You better believe we can. Even though we might be smaller than other companies you've worked with, I believe we can exceed your expectations, without question."

"Good... we were working with another company last year, but we didn't see the drive we see in you. Even though we serve a niche clientele, I think that..."

Henry spoke up rather suddenly, interrupting Mr. Williamson. It caught others off guard. "Who exactly is your clientele?"

The room became silent as all eyes were fixed on Henry. Even Rufus looked up from his notes as he looked over at his employer. A bit of tension filled the air as everyone waited for what Mr. Williamson would say next. He leaned back in his chair and pressed his fingers together. It was obvious that he was thinking intently about how to answer. "Our clients are those who are not known commonly by the public. They ship goods internationally and up the coast in freighters, mostly for private, single operator companies. We have also dealt with two international governments that supply inventory to others."

This was not the reply Damien was expecting. He still had lots of questions, but the mention of governments supplying inventory excited him. It meant that this deal was larger than anything he had expected. And it meant that this deal involved even more money than he had anticipated.

Henry continued with his questions, being very direct. "What exactly do you ship?"

Mr. Williamson shrugged his shoulders. "Anything really. Whatever our clients ask us to ship."

"How large are the quantities?"

"They vary dramatically. Sometimes we ship a single prized possession that is wanted from a buyer. It could be worth hundreds of thousands of dollars in and of itself. On the other hand, there are also large shipments sent out."

Henry leaned back in his chair and rubbed his chin. He thought carefully about the answers given from Mr. Williamson. The conversation continued on into the evening for another hour. The clock showed that it was approaching seven o'clock. Damien and Rufus seemed to be going strong in their exploration of the company. Henry could tell from Damien's body language that the more they discussed, the more excited he was about the deal.

When the clock struck exactly seven, Henry spoke up again. "Well... I think we have a lot of the information we need."

"Good," Mr. Williamson, whispering under his breath.

"But if you wouldn't mind, I'd like to take a recess and discuss the matter with my partner and lawyer. Possibly grab a bite to eat as well."

"It's no problem. We can have food brought in," Mr. Williamson objected.

"No... that's ok. I would really like to just speak with our gentlemen privately. We'll probably just clear our heads, talk through where we're at, and then reconvene." Henry paused briefly and looked up at the clock, "Say... 7:45? Unless that's too late for you fellows?"

Mr. Williamson bit his lip as he thought about what Henry was proposing. Eventually, he shrugged his shoulders. "Sounds fair enough. Where do you think you'll be?"

"Oh… probably nowhere in particular." Henry looked off to the side toward the ocean as he spoke. "I imagine we'll just grab something quick to eat and then take a walk by the ocean and discuss matters. I love the beach."

Damien turned abruptly to his partner. He knew something was amiss.

Chapter 7

Henry, Damien, and Rufus walked along the beach, their coats taken off and in their arms. They had started walking casually away from the resort. They were going toward the northwest, in the direction of St. Kitts. The further they walked, the more populated the beach became. Their mood was quiet as both Damien and Rufus knew that Henry had something on his mind he wanted to discuss. So far, he had said nothing as he made his way down the shore.

Damien was the first to speak about anything substantial. "A lot of information to think about. I think we all would agree this is a bigger deal than any of us thought."

"You can say that again. Definitely not what I was expecting," Rufus added.

"The way they want to expand would make this a very lucrative deal. If we can execute and find them the right clients, then I think we are in for a journey we've never dreamed of."

Henry simply smiled in return as he kept walking. He didn't say much, he just kept rubbing his chin, thinking. His walking pace began to be a little faster as they made their way up the beach. Damien could tell he was deep in thought.

It was then after fifteen minutes that Henry turned sharply away from the coast toward the interior of the island and the main road. "Let's head this way," he said quietly.

They crossed the road and walked toward a small convenience store that was stationed by the main road. "What are we doing?" Damien said, following Henry toward the store.

When they arrived in the parking lot, Henry stopped and pulled out his phone. "I'm calling for a cab," Henry said.

"What! Henry, what are you talking about? Where are we going?" Damien said, surprised.

"We have to get out of here right away." There was firmness in his voice.

"Wait. You've got to slow down." Damien put his hand on his business partner's wrist. "You're got to talk to me, man. Why the urgency?"

Henry looked up from his phone and directly at Damien. "The urgency is because of that meeting we just had."

"What do you mean?"

Henry was wide-eyed as he spoke directly to his partner, "Damien, don't be so naïve. Did you hear what they were saying? They weren't able to discuss specifically the contents of the shipments, and most of the companies they work with are not known to the public. What do you think that means?"

Damien tried to calm his partner. "Ok... I know what you're referring to, but I think..."

"It's obvious. They're working with black market goods." Henry was on the verge of shouting. "Everything about this smells of criminal activity."

Damien shook his head as he spoke, "No, you don't know that for sure."

"Oh, yes I do! Damien, I've been in business long enough to know that these are not the people that we want to be in contact with."

Damien rolled his eyes. "I think you're jumping the gun. We don't have nearly enough information to make a judgment call like that. We've only met with them for less than three hours and, besides, they want..."

"He's right." Rufus said, interrupting Damien. Henry and Damien turned to face him. He continued, "Henry's right, that is. I looked over all their documents thoroughly and everything is shrouded in secrecy. Also, there are other items that appear to be purposely hidden. It doesn't look good... at all."

"I can't believe this!" Damien was now angry. He put his hand on his forehead and paced slightly. Henry then went back to his phone and began calling the cab. Damien knew he had to act now. "Ok... hold on, Henry," he said, turning back to him. "Let's think this through, before you make this call."

Henry put down the phone, slightly frustrated. "I'm listening."

"I know there are some red flags, but let's just go back into that room and ask them openly and honestly about these concerns. What's the harm?"

Henry took a deep breath. "Damien... I'm going to be completely honest with you. From a business standpoint, their company is so much bigger than us that they could easily entangle us in transactions that are unethical, and besides, these guys are dangerous."

Damien was so upset. "Henry, this is crazy. We need this deal. I need this deal. How can you even start saying things like this over just one meeting?"

Looking around to his left and right, Henry checked to make sure no one else was listening in. He took a step closer to Damien. He was in his face. "Listen to me very carefully," he spoke quietly. "Their majority owner..."

"Yes, Lex Williamson."

Henry shook his head, "No, that's not his name."

"What are you talking about?

"His name is Alex Wellington. He's a fugitive, sought by the FBI."

"What are you talking about?"

"A few years back, he was suggested to have been involved in a conspiracy in a small town in Illinois. I remember the news reports vividly because the case was so odd. He was never found. With a simple search, I was easily able to find a photo of him online." Henry pulled up the search window on his phone and showed it to Damien.

Damien grabbed the phone and looked at it carefully. The man's hair was kept longer in the picture and there was no beard. "Ok, I see a resemblance, but still I don't think this is enough to say for certain. Let's at least go back into the meeting and ask more questions. Maybe more direct questions." Damien paused a moment, closing his eyes and wiping a little sweat off his forehead. He was very frustrated. He wanted Henry to think about what he was saying. The size of this deal would mean success. It would mean victory and prestige. At this point in his life, he needed it badly. "Please, Henry… one more meeting, that's all I'm asking."

Henry put his hand on Damien's shoulder, trying to calm his partner. He knew Damien was disappointed and had been through a lot lately. He so greatly wanted him to understand his concerns. Henry spoke as sincerely as he could. "Damien, I want to be as clear as I can." He paused for a moment to gather his thoughts. He took a deep breath before continuing, "There's no way I'm going back into that meeting. These guys are dangerous. I suggest we get on the 8:00pm ferry and take it back to St. Kitts and fly out as soon as we can. In fact, maybe even tonight."

Damien's face was clinched with anger. He'd never been so mad at Henry. "This is the dumbest decision you've ever made. All I want is for the three of us to head back into that meeting and just hear them out." Damien's anger was boiling over, making him a little out of control. "And this time, I'm making this decision, and you guys are going to like it."

Rufus stepped forward and spoke up as clearly as he could. "I'm not going back into a meeting with those guys. I've seen enough. I'm not messing around with them." There was great concern in his voice. Nothing would persuade him otherwise.

Damien was stunned. Rufus was usually up for a little risk. He had been hopeful that he could've at least convince the young lawyer to join him. Now, he didn't know what to do. He felt like shouting. He felt like cursing.

"I'm sorry, Damien," Henry said quietly, dialing the number for the cab. "We must leave now."

Even though Damien was furious, he knew he'd have to submit to their wishes.

The three men were on the ferry as it pulled out of the dock back toward the island of St. Kitts. It was a higher-end passenger ferry that specifically catered to tourists. It could accommodate around fifty, but currently it was less than half full. The helm of the boat was up a flight of steps to a room where the captain sat and steered. Underneath the helm was an enclosed cabin where passengers could sit in case of inclement weather. Overall, the boat was a little nicer than others, but still nothing fancy. For the moment, it definitely suited Henry's needs of getting them off Nevis and back to St. Kitts.

Originally, their plan was to ride back on the later ferries or possibly even one of *Worldwide Pathways'* private boats. Now with Henry's decision, everything had changed. Henry was currently on the phone talking with the airport, searching for a late flight out. So far, the search didn't look promising. His best bet at this point would be to wait and find an early flight out the next morning. It didn't matter where their flight was to. He just knew that they needed to get off these islands as soon as possible.

Damien was looking out onto the ocean, trying to settle his nerves. He felt like he was making the worst decision of his life. As a company, they had worked hard for over a year at getting this deal with *Worldwide Pathways*, and now they were seeing it all fall by the wayside simply because of Henry's suspicion. In the midst of all the pain Damien had endured over the last three weeks, the promise of this meeting was the one thing in life he had to look forward to. The disappointment of losing Lucy was softened in his mind with the potential of this deal being completed. It wasn't the money so much as it was the promise of greater things in store, greater things for the company, and greater things for his life and career. It was all gone now, simply because of a hunch by Henry. This was not the direction he was hoping for when they left North Carolina.

Thoughts of leaving *Parker & Wheaton* crossed his mind. In the past some of Henry's conservative business approaches got on his nerves, but it was never anything that made him think about leaving. Breaking this current deal was more than Damien could bear. He wondered...if he did leave the company, if he could then try to rekindle the agreement with *Worldwide Pathways*. He could only hope. Working with only their contract would be enough to compensate for what he was already making at *Parker &*

Wheaton. Many details would have to sorted through, but the idea sounded promising.

Rufus approached him and leaned against the railing beside him. "Hey, Damien," he said quietly. If there was one person Damien definitely didn't want to talk to, it was Rufus. On a scale of animosity, Rufus ranked even higher than Henry. Without Rufus confirming Henry's suspicion, the meeting would probably have continued. Damien figured if the young lawyer would have taken his side, then possibly they could've persuaded Henry to at least hear what *Worldwide Pathways* and Lex Williamson had to say about their concerns. Damien said nothing in reply to Rufus.

Rufus took off his glasses and held them in his hands. He continued, "Look, I know you're mad at me, but listen, I saw things in those files that brought me way too much concern. Henry's right. We don't want anything to do with those guys."

Damien shook his head as he bit down hard on his lip. He didn't make eye contact, but instead just continued looking stoically out into the water as he spoke. "You could've at least gone in there and asked them about your concerns."

Rufus closed his eyes. He felt a little embarrassed before his employer. "I'm sorry, Damien, but I did go over those papers thoroughly, and it was..."

"There's no way you could've read through all of them in that amount of time, especially in the midst of a meeting. I don't care how good you think you are. It's not happening."

Rufus brushed aside his brown bangs, purely out of nervousness. Talking to his boss like this made him uncomfortable. And naturally the fact that he was nine inches shorter than Damien brought another level of uneasiness. He would have to proceed with caution. "Listen, I definitely saw enough to come to a conclusion. I think Henry's right to bail on them. We don't even want to…"

"Wait! What?" Damien interrupted. He turned to face Rufus. He couldn't contain himself. "We're just bailing on them? Henry didn't even inform them that we weren't coming back?"

"Well… yeah," Rufus said. "We don't want to cross paths with these guys in any way. It's dangerous, man."

"I can't believe this." Damien said as he hit the railing with the palm of his hand. He knew he had to walk away before his anger kept boiling over. If he were to later reach out to *Worldwide Pathways* on his own, then he would now have this obstacle to overcome. He didn't want to hear anything from Rufus. He was done with this. Damien walked toward the front of the boat. He'd noticed a Coke vending machine when they first spotted the ferry.

"Where are you going?" Rufus called out.

"I need a drink."

The man called Lex Williamson stared out onto the beach from the outdoor meeting area on the Nevis resort. The sun was starting to set. He had a glass in his hand, filled with scotch. It helped to relax him. Most of the time he was patient, but currently he could feel anxiety rising within him.

The sudden departure of the men from the meeting was weighing on his mind. He was a man of power and authority. He hated when he lost control of situations.

Glancing down at his watch, he saw that it was now past 8:00pm. Too much time had passed since the three men left the meeting. Something was wrong. He was officially worried. Fifteen minutes ago, he had commissioned his men to search the island for Henry Wheaton and Damien Parker. His hope was that they were having dinner somewhere, simply discussing the terms of their agreement.

He wondered if he'd been too hasty in bringing this meeting together. He and his associates had researched *Parker & Wheaton* thoroughly, and found their aggressive approach to marketing and finding clients appeasing. From their track record it looked like they were a company that would do whatever it took to get the job done. Lex thought they would be a perfect fit, but as of right now he was starting to regret that decision. Now, he figured he might have a problem on his hands. A problem that would need to be taken care of.

"Sir!" a voice called out behind him. It sounded urgent.

Lex turned to see one of his associates. "Yes? Have you found them?"

"We have. They were spotted a few minutes ago getting on a ferry back to St. Kitts."

Lex clinched his fist in anger. "Are you sure it was them?"

"Positive." The young associate came forward with a file and handed it to his boss. "These were just sent over to me a few minutes ago. I printed them out." Opening it up, Lex Williamson saw photos of the men on the ferry on the port at Nevis. There was now no mistaking that he had a problem on his hands.

"Imbeciles!" he shouted out, throwing the file onto the table. "How long has it been since the boat left the dock?"

"Not long, they got on the boat early, but it just pulled out."

Lex cursed loudly. "We must get to them before the boat arrives at St. Kitts. You know what to do."

"Yes, sir. We're already on it," the associate said before walking away.

Lex gritted his teeth as he thought about Damien and Henry getting away. No one did this to him. He would do whatever it took to make sure his business was not compromised.

≪⋙

Damien stood on the front end of the ferry boat. He was looking at the choices of the drinks offered. He was trying to do anything to distract his mind from the business deal they had just walked away from. The vending machine read two dollars for a bottle of soda. He took out his wallet and inserted two bills. He pushed the button for Coke. One fell to the bottom as usual.

Grabbing the bottle, he opened it and took a sip. It was cold and was just what he needed at a time like this. He took a deep breath and leaned his head against the machine, trying to stay calm, settle his anger. "One step at a time," he whispered to himself. In his mind he just needed to get home and then he could work on repairing the deal. He could do this... he just needed to get back home first.

As he started to walk away from the machine, he was greatly startled. He dropped his bottle of Coke. Something had struck the boat.

Chapter 8

Damien ran to the back of the boat. His suspicions were correct. A smaller boat had run up beside the ferry and bumped it. Two men were climbing onto the ferry from the smaller vessel. They were dressed in suits with masks over their faces. They both had guns. As Damien got close, one started firing into the air. "Nobody move!" one shouted. The small crowd was startled by the gun shots. Many of them screamed out in horror.

"There he is, grab him!" one of the men shouted. He pointed at Henry through the crowd.

"Let's go," the criminal said as he grabbed Henry by the arm. He was pulling him in the direction of the smaller boat. Henry followed along willingly, hoping they would hurt no one.

The masked man in charge began shouting more commands and pointing the gun at the crowd. "Cooperate and nobody gets hurt!" Many in the crowd continued to cry out in horror and disbelief for what was occurring. Some shielded their eyes from the terror of the gun that was pointed their way.

The masked man continued, "I'm looking for three men. All dressed in suits. One is black and the other two are white." No one said a word. Most were too scared to speak. "Answer me, or I'll start firing," he shouted in a New England accent.

Judging by the fact that the masked men had taken Henry, Damien figured that they were looking for him. He reasoned in his mind that Henry's suspicions were correct. *Worldwide Pathways* were indeed corrupt, and this was most likely the consequence of Henry rejecting the deal with them. He knew he didn't have much time and he didn't want anyone to get hurt, so he stepped through the crowd toward the masked man. "I'm here," he said soberly.

"Get over here!" the masked man shouted. He grabbed Damien by the arm. "Where's the lawyer?" he shouted.

"I... I don't know." Damien said, scanning the crowd.

"Call him out," the masked man said forcibly to Damien.

Damien was frozen. He tried to weigh the consequences of what the masked man was asking. He didn't want Rufus to be captured, yet he also didn't want these men to start firing into the crowd.

"Do it, now!"

Damien thought it best to submit to the demands. "Rufus!" He waited a moment before calling again, "Rufus!" He scanned the crowd again. No one moved. "I don't see him. Maybe he's..."

Damien wasn't able to finish because at that moment he saw Rufus spring from behind a bench and ram the man that was pulling Henry toward the smaller boat. The masked man dropped his gun before hitting the railing and flipping over into the water. Rufus quickly picked up the gun and aimed it at the driver of the smaller boat. The driver was startled by this development and quickly drove off in the direction of Nevis.

The masked man holding onto Damien loosened his grip and pointed his gun in the direction of Rufus and Henry. Damien knew this was his opportunity. He grabbed the masked man by the arms and pulled him to the deck. The man was able to get one shot off toward Henry and Rufus as he fell. Damien held the man's arm with the gun against the ground. A senior fisherman from the crowd saw what was transpiring and came forward to help hold the masked man down. Damien then quickly removed the mask from the man. He then reared back and delivered a hard punch directly to the face of the man.

"Aww!" the man yelled in pain. Damien didn't wait more than a second or two before delivering another punch to the man's face. The masked man tried to pull and twist free from Damien and the fisherman. It was futile as Damien was not letting up. Damien then delivered another punch to the man's face, and then another. With each punch the man moved less and less. Slowly his grip on the gun eased up and the fisherman was able to get it out of his hands. Blood was now flowing from the man's nose, and bruises were starting to form. Damien got off of him when he thought he was fully unconscious.

Damien heard Rufus calling out about forty feet away. "Damien, I need help over here now!"

He turned to the fisherman, "Watch him. Keep the gun pointed on him." He didn't want any chance of the criminal waking up and coming after him.

Reaching Rufus, he saw Henry lying on the ground, holding his side. He was moaning in anguish. "What happened?" Damien said, with great concern in his voice.

"The other terrorist guy fired a shot, and... and... and it hit Henry right in the side." Rufus was starting to panic and go into shock at what had just occurred.

"Keep pressure on that wound," he instructed Rufus.

Damien then took off his suit coat and folded it over, making a pillow for Henry. He slid it under Henry's head. "Here you go, Henry. Try not to move too much."

Henry nodded in response. His body was shaking slightly. Damien feared he was losing too much blood. He knew he needed help. He called out to the crowd. "We need help over here! Is there a doctor present?" The small group of about twenty passengers were all basically gathered in one area. They still looked frightened. He looked back and forth among their faces, seeing if anyone in the group would respond. So far, no one was moving. He tried again, "Can anyone help?"

A few seconds passed before a dark-skinned woman in her mid-thirties from St. Kitts stood to her feet. She was with her husband and young son on the ferry. She said a few words to her husband before moving toward Damien.

"Are you a doctor?" Damien asked.

"No, but I am an emergency nurse," the woman responded. Her island accent was heavy.

"Good," Damien quickly led her toward Henry who was still lying on the ground.

As they came close to Henry, Rufus started frantically telling the nurse what he knew. "He's been hit on his side. I think the bullet went right through him. He's bleeding badly. I've been holding pressure on the wound. He's in his mid-sixties, and I'm scared he might lose consciousness and…"

"Shh, thank you," she said to Rufus. She recognized that Rufus was losing control of himself and didn't want the bad news he said to send Henry into a terrible shock. The nurse then went quickly to work, accessing the situation that lay before her. After a few seconds she looked up at Rufus to give him instructions, "There should be some type of first aid kit in the captain's cabin. See if you can find it."

"Ok," Rufus said, nodding. He quickly got up and ran in the direction of the captain's cabin.

Damien's mind seemed to be moving a mile a minute. He wondered if there was something else that he needed to do at that moment. He looked back at the fisherman still looking over the terrorist, who lay on the ground

102

unconscious. Now that Henry was being taken of, he thought he ought to check on that situation. "I'll be back," he said to the nurse. "Take good care of him." As Damien was about to leave, he noticed that beside the nurse, Rufus had left the gun. It appeared to be some type of revolver. Damien knew that it shouldn't be just lying around. He picked it up and stuck it in his belt.

He ran back toward the fisherman. He was a man who looked to be in his early seventies, but he was still in good physical shape. Damien also noticed another younger man of Asian descent was helping to watch over the unconscious criminal. The fisherman still held the gun in hand, just in case the criminal awoke. Both men looked anxious but kept their poise. "Any movement?"

"No... nothing," the Asian man said. "He's still breathing though."

"Good," Damien said under his breath. "Keep watch over him just in case he wakes up. My business partner took a bullet to his side. I'm going to keep helping with him." Damien looked back over his shoulder in the direction of the St. Kitts nurse. "I'm Damien, if you need anything just call out."

"Ok, thanks. We got this guy," said the fisherman.

Damien was about to head back to Henry, when he felt the boat take a sudden turn to the northeast and appear to speed up. It was passing between the two islands. He wondered what was transpiring. Rufus ran past him at this point. He had a first aid kit in hand. Damien quickly ran up the steps to the captain's quarters in search of more information. There was a single captain, a local man from St. Kitts. He was of African heritage in his mid-fifties. Opening the door to the cabin and stepping in, Damien could tell he was extremely nervous.

Damien spoke with great urgency, "We've got a man shot. We've got to get him to the hospital right away. Why the sudden change of direction?"

"Another boat was coming towards us from St. Kitts. It didn't look good."

"Could it have been someone to help us?" Damien said, turning aside to look behind him.

"No, definitely not," the captain's accent was thick. Damien had to listen closely to follow what he was saying. "These are more hostile characters. I could tell they mean us harm."

Damien didn't wait to hear anything else. He flung himself back outside the door and toward the passenger area of the boat. He quickly descended the steps and began yelling out, "Get down, everybody! Get down!" More of the people screamed out in horror as Damien yelled this warning. They all obeyed upon first command. Many slid themselves under the benches of the ferry.

As Damien reached the bottom of the steps, he heard a round of gunfire coming upon them. He jumped to the ground and put his hands over his head. "God, help us... help us," he prayed frantically.

He listened carefully as he heard the gunfire stop. He could hear the screams of the people and the boat coming closer. He lifted his head and looked around, accessing the situation. His mind went to the gun on his belt. He knew he couldn't just let the boat come upon them. He would need to go on offense. His instincts as a Marine kicked in. Damien quickly rose to his knees and looked over the bench that was in front of him. He could see the boat coming toward them about thirty yards away. Pulling the gun from his belt, he made sure the safety was off. He quickly yelled out, "Everybody, stay down!" He then fired off three shots from the handgun. More of the people screamed out in fear.

Damien ducked under the bench again as another round of gunfire was fired upon them. Same as before, Damien waited until it stopped and then fired three more shots toward the boat. These were the gun's last three bullets. He didn't know what he hit, but apparently it worked this time. He could see the boat veer off course from their pursuit. From behind the bench, Damien kept watch around it, but a full five minutes passed before he felt comfortable standing to his feet and moving about the ferry.

Assessing the situation, Damien could see only one criminal boat. It was fading into the distance as they were stopped to pick up their comrade who had fallen into the ocean from Rufus's hit. Looking around the ferry, he could see the people still on the ground, huddling. A few were stirring slightly. He noticed the fisherman with the gun in his hand was back watching the criminal again. The criminal was still sprawled out and bleeding, just as Damien had left him. He then looked over to the nurse who was crouched low, but working on Henry with the first aid kit. Rufus was by her side.

Damien wondered who he should check on first. The sun was now completely set and clouds were rolling in. A very light rain descended upon them. None of this mattered to him at the moment. He knew there was much to do. He first walked over to the passengers.

"Is everyone all right?" he announced. Some of the people started to rise. There were a few lights on the boat, where the passengers could assess their situation.

"Yeah, I think we're mostly fine," the nurse's husband responded.

"What's happening to us? Where are we going?" a woman asked.

Damien continued to check his surroundings. "I don't know. The captain was getting us away from those oncoming boats. We turned north."

"Who were those men that were after you?"

Damien didn't answer. He didn't know what to say or how he could explain everything so quickly. Instead, he walked over toward Henry and the nurse. She was still applying pressure to the wound, but this time with a bandage. "How is he?" he asked the nurse.

The nurse tilted her head to the side. "He's stable," she said professionally. "I think the bleeding has slowed a little, but we will need to get him to a doctor soon."

Damien bent down and put his hand on Henry's shoulder. "Hang in there, Buddy," he said softly. Henry reached up and grabbed Damien's hand. His face was clinched in pain. Damien had to look away. It was difficult to see his partner in this position.

"Damien," Rufus spoke up.

"Yes?"

Rufus stared out to the ocean. "Do you... do you know where we're going?"

Damien looked up to see the boat was headed toward a dense fog to the north. Because it was getting darker, their vision was already impaired. If they entered that fog, then visibility would be basically gone. Both of the criminals' boats were now completely out of sight, but he thought this route was still a bad idea because they wouldn't be able to see if another boat was coming up onto them. "I'll check with the captain," he responded.

He quickly left and headed back toward the captain's cabin. The passengers were beginning to move around the boat cautiously. Rain was starting to fall harder. A violent storm was coming. Damien ran up the steps and entered the captain's cabin. The captain was still at the controls keeping a watch on the ocean in front of him.

Seeing Damien, he began speaking. "I've been calling for help. The Federation authorities are well aware of our distress."

"Are they coming?"

"I let them know about the terrorists on the water. They're going to proceed with caution. There's also a storm coming on us quickly from the west."

"Ok," Damien turned and looked out the window, just to make sure the criminals were no longer following. He continued, "Do you think it's a good idea to head into that dense fog?"

"No, but I can't help it." the captain said, shaking his head. "When they fired upon us they must've hit the rudder or something in our steering system. The vessel's not moving like it should. We're also losing oil. Hopefully I can steer it enough to land back on St. Kitts."

Damien rubbed the top of his head, trying to stay focused, trying to think about what to do next. He wondered how much of this information should be reiterated to the other passengers. Rightfully so, many of them were still worried about the criminal boats coming back. He didn't want a panic to arise about their situation, but he knew they would be asking him for more information. "What should I tell the passengers?"

The captain did not break his focus. "Tell them to hold on… and pray."

"Ok," Damien said quietly as he turned to leave the cabin. He knew they were in for a long night.

Chapter 9

The boat was violently tossed along in the water. Lightning flashed, and thunder roared as the waves jostled the vessel up and down, and back and forth. Two hours had passed since the attack from the smaller boats. The storm had grown worse and worse over the past couple of hours. At this point the captain had almost lost all control of any steering. Their vision was also completely impaired as the fog had long overtaken them. The captain's hope was that the storm would pass, and the fog would clear up and from then they could assess their bearings and make landfall. They had drifted so far off course that the captain wondered if they were near Barbuda.

Currently, Damien was with all the other passengers in an indoor cabin. Many of the passengers sat on the benches calming their loved ones. Some of them had been staying on the island of Nevis and they were returning to St. Kitts and had their luggage beside them on the seats. Damien did what he could to try keeping them calm amidst the storm. Including the captain, there were twenty-three people total on the boat.

The fisherman, along with the Asian man, were still watching over the criminal. While helping to move the man earlier, Damien was able to deduce that the Asian man was the fisherman's son-in-law. The fisherman's name was Ron, and his son-in-law's name was Sean. They were on a fishing trip together on the island of Nevis and were on the ferry to St. Kitts to fly home the next day. Currently they had the criminal tied up with a rope and fishing line. He was stirring a little, and moaning on occasion, but overall, he was basically still unconscious. Ron had the gun in hand, just in case the criminal woke up. That was a situation Damien wasn't worried about.

The St. Kitts nurse was still taking care of Henry. The medical kit she was working with was more extensive than a traditional first aid kit. Though more work needed to be done at the hospital, she felt as if she was able to thoroughly clean the wound and get the blood flow slowed. She gave him 1500 milligrams of acetaminophen, but even still the pain was strong. As the boat tossed back and forth along the waves, certain bumps of the boat would jostle Henry, causing him severe pain. He would cry out in anguish. Hearing Henry's cries but not being able to help him was possibly the most difficult part for the passengers.

Rufus approached Damien, still worried. "Do you think Henry's going to make it?"

"Yes," Damien said with no hesitation in his voice. "All we need to do is get him to a hospital. He'll be fine."

At that moment the boat hit a violent wave and both men stumbled. The shifting moved Henry and he let out another cry of pain. Damien and Rufus both grabbed ahold of a nearby bench to steady themselves. Lightning continued to flash, and thunder continued to rumble. Rufus continued, "I just hope you're right, man." He ran his fingers through the top of his hair. "I keep wondering if I did the right thing in pushing the other guy off. Maybe they would have just taken us back to Nevis. Maybe Henry wouldn't have gotten shot. Maybe we could've..."

"No, don't do that, Rufus," Damien quickly interjected. "They had guns pointed at us. We don't know what they were planning to do to us or the other passengers. You did what was right."

Rufus began to cry. The emotions of the whole evening were catching up with him. He couldn't hold back. The tears were flowing strong. He spoke through his crying breaths, "I just... don't want him to die, not now. Especially after everything you've been through lately with your wife and daughter and all. I know it'd be too much for you too, and... "

Damien grabbed ahold of Rufus' arm and pulled him closer. A serious look was on his face. He spoke forcibly, "Rufus! You've got to pull yourself together. We can't do this now. We've got to focus on getting out of this storm and getting these people to safety. You hear me?"

Rufus' face was down as he was still crying. All he could do was nod in response to Damien's question.

"All right, stay strong. I need you in this," Damien said to him. Rufus continued to sniff from the crying. "You've got to hold it all in. There's no time for you to be crying like this. Hold it in… hold it in."

Rufus took a deep breath and nodded one more time for Damien. "Ok, I can do this," he said hesitantly.

"Atta boy," Damien responded, patting him on the arm. "I'm going to check again with that elderly couple, make sure they're doing ok. Stay strong… stay strong."

Lex Williamson had twenty of his associates and henchmen gathered around a table. They were inside the resort in Nevis. Lex stood while all the others were seated, "Imbeciles! How could you have let them get away?"

One of his men spoke up timidly, "They threw one of our men overboard, and were able to knock down the other. We weren't aware that they may fight back."

"Weren't aware! Weren't aware," Lex was wide-eyed, and his blood was boiling. Anger consumed him, overwhelmed him. "You're supposed to be ready for any situation! Why didn't you go after them with another boat?" No one said a word as they all were afraid of Lex. "Answer me!" he shouted.

"We... we tried," another associate spoke up. "They turned off course and began firing at us. One of the bullets struck our boat and we turned away."

"Aww... madness," Lex pulled his hair in frustration. He couldn't believe they had given up so easily. "Do you realize the situation we are now in? I can't believe this." Using his cane for help, he took a seat on one of the chairs. He tried to relax himself. He reached forward and grabbed the glass of scotch in front of him. He focused hard on trying to stay calm. "Where are they now?"

"We actually don't know. We lost them as a storm came on. We fear they may have circled back around and made it to St. Kitts."

Lex hit the table hard with his fist. "Then what are you doing here? Find them!"

"But... but, sir, there is a violent storm out there. We need to..."

"I don't care!" Lex shouted. His face was strained. "Find them!"

❧❧

Another two hours passed. The ship was still being tossed along by the violent ocean. Damien occasionally checked his phone but found that they were way too far for any service. He continued to look around at the passengers, making sure everyone was fine. There was great anxiety among everyone, but thankfully no one was in an all-out panic.

A man in his early twenties was sitting beside Rufus. He was thin with long blond hair. It was obvious from the way he was dressed and the short board beside him that he was a surfer. In his nervousness, he pulled from his pocket a small white rolled up paper and stuck the end in his mouth. He took out a lighter with it.

Rufus looked over at him. "Are you sure that's a good idea?"

He shrugged his shoulders. "One life to live, bro... and it's lookin' like it might be about over."

The surfer guy tried to light up but before he could, Damien stopped him, grabbing the joint out of his mouth. He crushed it with his hand. "No, sir, not here. Not now," he said firmly.

He didn't even think about retaliating, but just laughed a little in response. "All right, whatever you say, dude. Just hopin' we get out of this mess."

"Yeah... we will. The storm should pass soon enough," Damien said, trying to sound as reassuring as he could.

His mind went to the captain. He wondered if he'd heard anything in the last few hours. It was still storming hard, but he figured he could be quick in running up the steps to the captain. "Stay here," he said to Rufus as he went to exit. All the others took notice and were a little shocked when they saw him leave the room. When Damien exited the indoor cabin, the rain hit him strong. He stumbled a little but purposed in his mind to keep moving. He turned to his right and ran up the steps. He didn't stop until he reached the captain's door. There was a strong strike of lightning as he opened the door and threw himself in. He could see the captain, still focused at the helm, trying to keep the boat steady, and looking on the horizon for a direction to head. He was a little surprised to see Damien enter.

"Anything, Captain?"

"Nothing yet, visibility is still low, but the fog is clearing slightly."

"Any signs of the weather clearing up?"

He shook his head. "Not yet at least. I'm just trying to stay steady. I've been doing this for twenty years and between the storm and the fog, I've never been in anything like this... bad luck."

The two men were silent for a minute as they watched the boat go up and down against the waves. Damien thought the captain's observation was correct, the fog was beginning to clear up just a little.

"How's the man who was shot?" the captain asked.

Damien shrugged his shoulders, "He's stable, but in pain. The rough waters are definitely not helping."

"I see, and what of the other passengers?"

"They're ok. Very shaken up."

"Well, they've been through a lot for one day."

The thunder continued to roar, and the lightning continued to strike. It was chaos, but in the midst of it the captain turned to Damien and spoke calmly without breaking his focus, "My name's Jones."

Damien chuckled a little at the irony of it. "Good to meet you, Captain Jones. I'm Damien." They didn't shake hands or even make eye contact as the captain was trying to stay focused. It was a very calm, ironic moment in the middle of the fierce storm. These two men felt an instant bond as they were both working to get the passengers back to safety. They were kindred spirits.

Knowing there was nothing else that needed to be done, Damien wanted to get back to the passengers. "Well, I should probably head back down to the people."

"Yes, Damien, thank you very much," the captain responded.

Damien went toward the door and was about to open it, when he thought of one last question. "Captain, what about the criminal boats? I don't know if you've heard or seen anything, but do you think we should be on alert in case they come back after us?"

"Oh no, no, Damien," the captain said in his strong island accent. "Those boats aren't going to find us. We're way off course. Don't tell the others, but I have no idea where we are or what direction we're headed."

Damien didn't know what to say in response. They were deeper into trouble than he originally thought. He simply turned and left the cabin.

Julia awoke in the night. She slowly sat up. The house was dark. There was a little light coming in from the window. All was quiet. Her mother was staying in their guest room. She would be ready to help in an instant if her daughter needed anything. Julia was in some pain, but that is not what had awakened her.

She couldn't say exactly why, but she was suddenly worried for Damien. Looking at the clock, she could see it was past 2:00am. She didn't know what it was but her instinct told her that her husband needed help now. He had been on her mind all day, but this was different. There was something urgent that he needed help with at this moment.

Julia slowly climbed out of bed and did the same thing she always did when she knew he needed help. She prayed. Getting down on her knees she put her hands together and closed her eyes. "God, please help my husband. I'm not sure what's going on, but I know he needs you now. Give his mind clarity, help him to know what to do in the moment."

"God, I don't know if this is related to the loss of Lucy or not, but please continue to comfort him with her loss. Help him as he needs to open up about his pain." She brushed her hair out of her face and took a deep breath before continuing with the prayer. "And, God, thank you that you are leading us and guiding us. You are the Good Shepherd, and even with this pain we're going through, you have never left us or forsaken us. I pray these things in the name of the Father, Son, and Holy Spirit... Amen."

Julia gingerly rose to her feet. Even though she was still worried about her husband, she felt a sense of peace rush over her as she climbed back into bed.

The passengers aboard the ferry held each other tight. The waters were still rough, but the storm had greatly lessened. It was now after 5:00am and though everyone was still a little nervous about their situation, the tension had eased up slightly. Because of the storm's calming, Henry was no longer being jostled about, and as a result, he no longer cried out randomly in pain. This substantially helped everyone's mood on the boat.

Through the night Damien had helped to keep everything under control. The elderly couple, Milo and Gladys, had been the ones he most worried about. They both had endured a few bumps and bruises, but overall, they were fine. Rufus and the blond-headed surfer guy, Beck, had struck up a friendship, and they were now helping Damien with a few miscellaneous tasks. Damien was thankful Beck hadn't tried to light up a joint again during the night. The fisherman, Ron, and his son-in-law, Sean, were still watching over the criminal, except now he had awakened. He wasn't speaking coherently yet about who he was or what he was doing specifically, but more than anything, they were all anxious to get him to the authorities.

Damien had gone up to check on Captain Jones a couple more times through the night. He was straight forward with Damien every time that he didn't know their location. His hope was that they would have spotted Barbuda and somehow steered for it or radioed for help, but he knew their direction was now too far to the north to intersect the island. The steering on the boat was still not functioning properly. Captain Jones actually thought it had gotten worse as the rough night progressed.

The fog was just about gone, and the light of the sun could be seen slightly. Damien looked out onto the water and tried to see if there was any land or another boat that could be seen. He had mixed feelings about seeing another boat, as a part of him was worried that some of Lex Williamson's men might still be after them. He kept the gun close to him just in case they met more enemies.

He was deep in thought when the St. Kitts nurse interrupted him. "Damien," she said softly.

"Yes," he turned suddenly, a little shocked. Instantly, in his mind he became worried about Henry.

"It's ok," the nurse said, putting her hand up. "He's feeling much better now that the boat is no longer rocking."

"Good," Damien responded, calmer.

"My hope is that we can get him comfortable enough to sleep. The acetaminophen probably isn't providing much relief from the pain, but my hope is that any fever that may come on him may be lessened by the medicine."

"All right," Damien said, looking away. He wasn't sure what to ask or say. In fact, he wasn't even sure he wanted to know anything more. The idea of his friend being shot and in grave pain was a lot for him to bear. He didn't want to think about it and tried to suppress any thoughts that Henry's health may be threatened. He bit his lip as his emotions started to rise within him. He determined to hold it all in.

The nurse continued, "I'll keep you informed. You'll be the first to know if anything changes drastically."

"Thanks," Damien said. He peeked over at Henry lying on the deck. His coat was still used as a pillow, but now he also had a blanket over him. Damien could see him breathing. He hoped his friend could get some sleep.

"Damien," a voice said to his right.

He turned to see it was Rufus. "Yes, Rufus." He could see the young lawyer was looking out onto the horizon in front of them.

"I think I see something in front of us... it may be land." Damien looked out and, sure enough, he could see what appeared to be small mountains in the distance. He looked closely, studying the scene in front of him. He hoped that what they were seeing was correct, and that his eyes weren't playing tricks on him. Others saw Rufus and Damien looking on the horizon and followed suit, studying the scene from afar. The passengers began talking among themselves as the hope of landfall was finally in front of them. Many rose from their seats and went toward the window in order to get a better glimpse.

"Stay here," Damien said to Rufus. He quickly exited the room. He needed to speak with the captain. He ran up the steps toward the captain's cabin. Before entering, he stopped and took another look at the sight in front of them. It was clear, and at this point there was no denying that a mountainous island was in front of them. With the present condition of the boat's steering, he hoped the captain could make for it.

He opened the door and went in. He didn't bother with pleasantries as his curiosity was boiling over. "Can we make that island?"

"Yes... yes... I think so," Captain Jones responded. "It's a little off the course we're going, but I think I can steer it just enough to head straight toward it."

"Have you tried radioing to it?"

"Yes, but no response so far."

Damien nodded in response. He took out his cellphone, but still there was no reception, and in fact the battery was almost dead at this point. He turned it off, just in case he would need it later. He continued addressing the captain, "Well... keep trying. Surely someone will eventually hear."

"I will," the captain said, without breaking focus.

The light of the sun continued to increase, and the fog had now completely cleared. Damien looked in every direction from the boat and could see nothing else besides the island in front of them. Through the night any bearings of direction he might have had were gone. He no idea and no guesses where they were.

Turning now and looking forward at the island again, he spoke to the captain, "Jones, may I ask what is that island we are moving toward?"

The captain sat in silence for a moment or two thinking through Damien's question and considering how to answer. In the end he thought he would just be honest. "Damien... I actually don't know. I've traveled far and wide through the Caribbean, and truthfully, I must say I've never seen it before in my life." He then paused for a moment, before speaking quietly, "Something's not right."

Damien took a deep breath. He wondered what they were headed into.

Chapter 10

It was after 6:00am and the boat was making its way to the land. They were close. The storm had now completely passed, and the sky was nearly cloudless. The passengers didn't speak much as they observed the island as it came closer. It was green and rich in vegetation. There was about twenty-five yards of sand between the water and where a forest started. From there one could see all sorts of trees, including a few palm trees close to the edge of the forest.

The island itself didn't look particularly large. One would guess the width was just over three miles. The length couldn't be seen from their perspective. The elevation on the island rose sharply from the beach since a small mountain range formed a wall on this side of the island. The passengers couldn't see where the mountains ended, but rather it appeared from their vantage point that they just continued wrapping around the island. There were no signs of inhabitants, just a few birds flying overhead.

Damien wondered what they would find once they landed. He found it curious that the captain didn't know what island this was. Since their vision had been impaired during the storm, Damien thought that possibly the boat was tossed even farther off course than the captain realized. Maybe they had drifted toward the southeast and now they were close to French-Guadeloupe.

Eventually, the boat ran ashore and stopped. The captain stopped the engine and many of the passengers exited the cabin room slowly. They were awestruck as they observed their surroundings. From their vantage point it looked to be a paradise island. Captain Jones then promptly exited his cabin and descended the steps. Reaching the boat's deck, he quickly threw an anchor from the side into the water.

As Damien walked the deck of the boat toward the sand, he looked around one last time just to make sure there were no boats following them. Seeing that everything was clear, he addressed those who were walking with him. "Does anyone recognize this island?"

The nurse's husband spoke up. He was also a St. Kitts native. "No, it's very curious. We must be far from our island." Others in the group spoke up as well, but none knew of their location.

Damien continued, "Well, I suggest we stay together. Help may be coming soon."

The captain approached those on the deck. At this point others had exited the indoor cabin area and were joining the group on the deck. "Is everyone all right?" Many nodded their heads in response. Everyone was still a little shaken up from being up all night and going through the rough waters. The elderly couple particularly was ready to be off the boat.

Damien turned to the captain. "Were you able to contact anyone over the radio?"

"No," the captain said, shaking his head. "I'll keep trying, but, so far, nothing yet."

"Ok," Damien said quietly. He rubbed the back of his neck as he thought about what to do. A part of him thought they ought to stay on the boat and just wait and see if help showed up soon. But another part of him thought they ought to move to the shore, just in case another rogue boat came upon them. They would be severely trapped if a large group of criminals ambushed them. Also, upon further thought, Damien thought it would lift the spirits of everyone to be off that boat after ten hours.

"Hey, everyone!" he said loudly. The passengers turned to face him. It was clear to everyone by now that he was their leader. He had been calm and kept his poise throughout the night. Most were ready and able to follow his lead. "I suggest we all move off this boat. It will do us some good. You can stay close to it on the beach if you want to keep your luggage on board." He then turned to his young lawyer, "Rufus!"

"Yes?"

"I want you to get everyone water and drinks from the machine."

"Oh... ok. I don't know if I have enough cash," he said, looking into his wallet for dollar bills.

"Rufus, just do what you can. You can probably check with the captain. He might have a way to open it."

The surfer Beck spoke up, "I'll help it with it." He spoke with a big smile on his face as he pulled Rufus toward the machine.

The nurse's husband addressed the crowd. "We have a few snacks and crackers if anyone is in need."

"We've got a few things as well," the elderly man Milo added.

"Good," Damien said. "We'll plan to keep our injured friend, Henry, on board. It's probably best if we move him as little as possible." He turned to Sean, who was listening to the instructions. "Do you think you and Ron could move our detainee onto shore?"

Sean shrugged his shoulders. "We'll try. He's been uncooperative so far. Where do you want him?"

Damien turned to observe the beach. He bit his lip as he tried to think of the best position. "Umm... just put him in the grass right where the sand stops."

"Ok," Sean responded, heading back to the cabin.

Damien looked toward the captain who was standing toward the back of the group. "Captain Jones!"

"Yes?"

"Do you have any instructions for us?"

The captain just looked off to the side as he thought about Damien's question. He wasn't sure what to say. Damien could tell there was something on his mind. After a few moments of silence, Damien spoke again, "Captain?"

He spoke quietly, "No." He was still looking toward the island, trying to observe it thoroughly. "But it might be best if we stay close to the boat," he added.

Damien was caught off guard by the captain's sudden timidity. He greatly wondered what he was thinking, but he knew this was neither the time or place to ask. He simply turned back to the crowd. "Ok... we'll do it. Please, let me know if anyone needs help."

The people then scattered. Many started gathering what belongings they had and moving onto the beach. For the most part, everyone was anxious to get off the boat. The captain, Henry, and the St. Kitts nurse were the only ones who were planning to stay on the boat. Everyone else was busy helping each other make the transition to the beach.

Through the crowd, Damien was able to observe the captain holding onto the railing, looking out to sea. Damien passed through the people to the captain. He could tell that there was still something prominent on his mind. "Captain?" He didn't respond. "Is everything ok?"

The captain shook his head. "Something is very odd."

"What do you mean?"

The captain didn't break his gaze, but just kept looking out to sea. "I don't know where we are, and surely an island this big I would have seen before. Something's not right... something's not right."

Damien didn't know how to respond. He found the captain's demeanor very strange. "Well," he said, looking back on the shore. "Keep trying the radio and seeing if you can get anyone in response. Hopefully, help will come soon."

The captain took a deep breath before speaking quietly. "Yes... I hope so... I hope so."

Throughout the morning the passengers spread themselves out along the beach. All were still relatively close to the boat's location. Some moved onto the grass by the wooded area where the sand stopped. Many tried to lie down and rest as the night had taken its toll on most. At first there was fear of an enemy boat approaching them, but as time passed that fear had subsided.

The passengers particularly kept a close eye on the elderly couple, Milo and Gladys. Currently, they were seated under a tree in the shade. Milo was a traveling preacher, and for the past couple of weeks, he had been on St. Kitts and Nevis speaking to different congregations and missionaries. Like others, they were traveling back to St. Kitts in order to fly out the next morning. They were tired and sore from the night, but overall, thankful for the help others had given them. They had a peace about them that was to be admired.

Rufus and Beck were supplying everyone with a bottle of water or a soft drink. In his younger years Beck had learned how to break into drink machines. After a few misdemeanors on his record, he decided to give up that life and try to go straight. And for the most part, besides being caught occasionally with marijuana, his life had stayed free of trouble. He had been on St. Kitts and Nevis for over a month, surfing and simply enjoying island life. There were no long-term plans in his life other than to stay clean and "hang loose." He was from Santa Monica, California, and had no plans to return.

The nurse had spent the morning getting her husband and son settled and attending to Henry. Her name was Elizabeth, and she had been a nurse for over ten years and was very gifted in the field. Many on the island of St. Kitts knew her and her story. She was born into poverty with many obstacles to overcome. Growing up, she was inspired by her mentors and she worked hard on her education. She eventually was able to leave the island and study nursing in Florida, only to return later to help her native people that she loved dearly. Currently, she was proving to be calm under pressure. The gravity of the situation with Henry didn't rattle her. She just kept working with him, trying to do whatever she could for her injured patient. Henry himself was still struggling greatly. Elizabeth's hope was that she could get him comfortable enough to sleep. As of right now that proved to be a challenge.

The fisherman Ron and his son-in-law Sean were the farthest from the boat up the shore. They had moved the criminal into the shade and made sure he was well tied up. An extra fishing line had been applied to his hands and feet. Ropes still confined his body. Besides pleas to be released and insults, the criminal wasn't saying anything helpful yet. Ron had spent some time in the Navy and was comfortable watching their criminal. For now, Damien had no reservations about Ron keeping the gun.

The other passengers were a mixture of St. Kitts natives and American tourists. There was a range of emotions among them. Some were staying calm and were just trying to stay comfortable and help their fellow passengers. Others were worried as they looked around and saw no one or no signs of life. Many of the people's cellphones had died by now, and most of the others had no signal. One American man claimed he was getting a faint trace of a signal, but soon found his hope in vain as he quickly lost it. At this point most had come to terms with the idea that trying to call for help was impractical.

After getting himself settled, Damien spent the majority of his time assessing their current situation and thinking through a plan of action. It was difficult as he couldn't even begin to guess when help may come. He wondered how much information had gone out concerning their disappearance. Damien checked with Captain Jones periodically to see if he knew any more information concerning their location, but he was still baffled as to where they were. Any attempt to contact people on the radio had also been in vain.

It was now getting close to noon. Rufus was passing by when Damien stopped him. "Rufus, is everyone still doing ok?"

He rubbed his forehead as he spoke, "I guess... we're keeping a close eye on the elderly couple. Just want to make sure they don't get too hot."

"Are they all right?"

Rufus nodded his head. "Yeah, they're fine. Just like everyone else they're anxious for a rescue boat to come."

Damien bit his lip as he looked out onto the sea. There was nothing on the horizon. A lot of the information and thoughts from Captain Jones came to mind. With their present unknown location, he wondered how long it would be exactly before they could reasonably expect help to come. He wondered if it would be another day or two, which if that was the case, then they had better formulate a longer-term plan. He took a deep breath before speaking to his young lawyer. "Rufus, I think we better call a meeting of everyone, and make a plan."

"A meeting? What do you mean?"

"I think we better get everyone together and relay all the information we know. Just to be sure we are all on the same page."

Rufus was confused. "Are you sure that's a good idea? Everyone's settled and just looking out for the rescue boats."

He hated to break this news to friend, much less everyone else. "Well... that's the thing, Rufus. I'm not sure how long it will be before one comes."

Rufus was taken aback. "What? Why?"

"According to Captain Jones, we're greatly far off course. He doesn't know where we are, and it may take a day or two before we are found."

Rufus took a deep breath. He hated hearing this news, but trusted Damien and knew there was a lot of truth to what he was saying. He quickly looked around to the others

130

scattered on the beach. "Ok, I would suggest we have everyone meet by the elderly couple, Milo and Gladys, so they don't have to move."

Damien rubbed the sweat off his head as he thought through this suggestion. It sounded reasonable enough. "All right. Let's plan to meet in about fifteen minutes. Do you think you can notify everyone?"

"Sure."

Chapter 11

The people readily agreed to the meeting. Milo and Gladys welcomed the prospect of staying where they were as the temperature was hot and their spot was very shady. Everyone was present except Henry and Ron. The nurse Elizabeth had given Henry another large dose of acetaminophen, and he was able to drift off to sleep. She felt she could spare a few minutes away to hear what the group would discuss. Ron was also not present as he stayed watching the criminal. The people were gathering together under the shade of the trees.

Seeing the people gathered, Damien addressed the group, "Ok, do we have everyone?" He looked around, making sure all were present. Out of habit, he checked his watch. It, of course, was still cracked and not working.

"Yeah," a couple of people responded.

Damien continued, "I know I've met mostly everyone, but I wanted to formally introduce myself. My name is Damien Parker, and, like a lot of you, I was visiting Nevis and was going back to St. Kitts to fly out the next morning." Damien made sure he projected his voice well. In no way did he want to come across as timid. "I wanted to get all of you together to make sure we're all on the same page and relay any information I knew." He paused a moment, glancing through the crowd. They all listened intently as they were hungry for information.

"I've been talking with the captain, and it appears from the storm and the fog that we have gone greatly off course. We're far from St. Kitts, and actually we're so far that the captain doesn't know our exact location." There wasn't much reaction from the crowd since rumors had been spreading and most knew this by now.

Sean was the next to speak, addressing the captain. "Have we been able to reach anyone on the radio?"

"No... no one at all," the captain said in his strong St. Kitts accent. "It appears we're far from any civilization." At this, a few looks of despair formed on the faces of the crowd. The news of how stranded they were was fully sinking in.

Damien continued, trying to sound hopeful. "I would imagine that by now search groups have probably been sent out from St. Kitts and possibly America, too. My suggestion to everyone would be to get comfortable and to help one another as it may be tomorrow or possibly the day after that before they find us."

"Do you really think it'll take that long?" another person asked.

Captain Jones spoke up. "I don't know. We are so far off course that Mr. Parker might even be optimistic in his timeframe. It could be longer." Damien was a little upset with this statement, wishing the captain would have first said this to him before announcing it to the group, or at least kept this news to himself.

"What do we do if it's longer?" said a panicked individual.

"Yeah, we could all die out here," added another.

Damien put his hands up. "Ok, let's all calm down a minute here and take a breath. We're going to get through this. We have to stick together and plan well. If we do that, then we should be fine."

Beck was lounging against a tree. "So, what's the plan, Chief?" he said with a smile on his face. He looked like the only one in the group enjoying himself.

"All right… here's what we're going to do. The captain will be on the boat most of the time, trying to contact anyone he can on the radio. Nurse Elizabeth will also be on board with Henry, trying to keep him comfortable and his fever down. I would suggest that we all try to stay off the boat for Henry's sake unless it's an emergency. Did anyone leave any luggage on board?"

No one said a word. Some shook their heads.

Damien continued, "Good. Tomorrow morning if no one's come, I'm going to journey up the mountains to see if I can see anything from up high and look for a fresh water source."

Beck sat up. "Chief, if you're going up to those mountains, then I'm coming too. Sounds like an adventure, dude."

"That's fine," Damien responded, knowing it was probably a good idea to take someone with him. He then pointed toward Rufus as he continued speaking to everyone, "My associate, Rufus, will be glad to help you if anyone needs anything while I'm gone."

Rufus was caught off guard. His eyes were wide. "Oh... ok... sure, I think I can do that. Yeah... I can."

Damien then looked toward Sean. "Do you think you and Ron could try to catch some fish for us?"

Sean chuckled a little to himself. "Absolutely. Ron can catch fish anywhere."

"Good. How is the prisoner? Do you need any help with him?"

"Hmm..." Sean rubbed his chin as he thought about what to say. "I don't know. He's fine for now, just angry, and acting a little strange."

Damien wanted to ask what he meant, but thought he ought not to chase that trail at the moment. "Ok... well, let us know if you guys need any help. Eventually, I would like to try to talk to him."

"Good luck with that," Sean said sarcastically.

Damien turned toward the group. "I think something we can also do is..."

"Excuse me!" an American woman interrupted.

"Yes?" Damien said, taken off guard.

The woman seemed a little upset. "I think there's something we're all wondering. Something you haven't addressed."

"Ok," Damien was intrigued. "And what may that be?"

"I think we're all wondering who were those guys that attacked us. Or I guess, more specifically, the ones who tried to attack *you*?"

Damien scratched the back of his neck as he thought about how to respond. He didn't want to get into detail about *Worldwide Pathways* and who they thought they were, or for that matter, who Lex Williamson was exactly. He tried his best to explain. He spoke a little softer. "I'm not entirely sure, but I imagine they were from this shipping company that my company was trying to do business with. The deal soured, and from what I guess, they were seeking to retaliate against me and my business partner, Henry."

Many of the people found this curious. Another person in the group spoke up, confused, "This came from a shipping company?"

Damien hesitated a moment before speaking. "Yes, it was a strange situation, but from what we can best guess, this shipping company deals with illegal black-market goods. They didn't like the fact that we didn't complete the deal with them."

Many of the group found this information enlightening. They asked a lot of questions concerning Damien's business and *Worldwide Pathways*. Damien didn't want to answer a lot of these questions and thought they were a waste of time, but more than anything, he thought he ought to answer some of their inquiries since his company was the reason they struck their boat. After a few minutes of questioning, the crowd had most of their questions answered and were satisfied. A few sounded upset with Damien, but most understood that there was nothing that could be done for now and that the best course of action was to keep moving forward.

Damien continued, "Ok, let's go ahead and get to work. I would advise everyone—if you don't have anything to do and feel like you have the strength, then I'd say venture into the edge of the woods and find any dry firewood you can. We're going to need it for tonight."

The group was beginning to stand and move out when Milo spoke out. "Excuse me... everyone." The group stopped and looked toward him. His voice was a little soft, but certainly distinct. "I think before we all disperse, we should have a word of prayer." Everyone was extra sensitive toward him and his wife, Gladys, as they realized their older age made this excursion roughest among all of them.

No one objected. He continued, "All right. Let's pray." He paused a moment for everyone to bow their heads. "Dear God, we come before you because we need your help this day. You have said in your Word that you are the Good Shepherd, and as the Good Shepherd you are leading us through life, walking right beside us."

As Milo continued to pray, Damien tried to zone out. The words Milo was praying struck a nerve with him. They were basically the same thing Pastor Thomas had said to him and Julia in the hospital after the loss of Lucy. The words didn't seem true, especially now. *Where was God when Henry was shot? Where was God when they were in the fog?* Now they were stranded and who knows what would happen next.

Milo was still praying. "Help us not to fear, even if we pass through the valley of the shadow of death, because you are with us. We pray these things in the name of the Lord Jesus, amen."

Damien turned abruptly and walked away from the group. The prayer had rattled him, and besides, there was much that needed to be done.

The sun was starting to set, creating a beautiful scene on the beach. If it had been just about any other situation, the people would have enjoyed it. Three fires were blazing strong along the beach. It had taken most of the afternoon to find dry firewood, but eventually enough was found to sustain three fires along with extra wood for fuel throughout the night. It was a lot of work to find all the wood, but as of right now, the people were greatly thankful they had spent the time finding it.

Some of the people were discouraged that there had been no sign of help yet. Even though they had heard the captain's information about how far they had drifted off course, many were still holding out hope that somehow, some way, help would come. A couple of people hadn't even bothered to help with the firewood, or even try to get comfortable as they were solely fixed on the idea of help coming soon. But now, even they were coming to the realization that they would be spending the night here on the island.

The people spread themselves out between the three fires. What little food they had was being shared and passed around among everyone. It consisted mostly of granola bars and crackers. Ron and Sean had caught a handful of smaller fish along the shore. Any other time they wouldn't have thought twice about throwing them back, but in this case, anything caught was welcome. They fileted the fish and were currently cooking the meat over the fire on sticks. Even though it was a small contribution, the people were thankful for it.

Currently, the people were relaxed around the fire, talking among one another about their lives and families. Beck could be heard the loudest among all the others. He spoke freely about his time on Nevis and about some of the adventures he'd had there. He then ventured into telling some of his various surfing stories. His laughter and smile were infectious. Without question he was the most relaxed in the group. Many found his demeanor calming to be around, while others thought his loud and boisterous voice was quite annoying. "Then after I finally got up on my board, a wave comes and wipes me out, boom, man! My nose lands hard on the board, and it starts to bleed. Your mind then goes to sharks, and..." He continued speaking freely.

Across the fire, the fisherman Ron was helping people cook the fish on the sticks. There were two children on the ferry that were now on the island with them, one from

America and the other from St. Kitts. Thinking it might cheer them up, Ron had let them cook a couple of his fish. He was gentle with them as they held their sticks over the fire. "Now, you don't want to hold the meat too close to the fire because it may catch on fire." He then gently grabbed the wrist of the St. Kitts boy and carefully adjusted his hands where they needed to be. "Right about there should be fine." The boy smiled in return. He was thankful for this little bit of fun amidst all the turmoil of this excursion.

At that time Gladys came by to warm her hands by the fire. She stood right beside Damien. Seeing her approach, he spoke up, "How have you been doing this evening?"

She smiled slightly. "Doing ok. Just a little cold."

"Still happy to be off the boat?"

She held up her hand and chuckled a little. "Absolutely... you can say that again." Earlier in the day she and Damien had a conversation, and she had told him in great detail how she wasn't fond of water. As difficult as this journey had been for her, more than anything she was thankful to be off the boat.

"How's Milo?" Damien asked.

"Oh, he's fine. Just tired. He'd been working hard, meeting with people and speaking this past week on St. Kitts and Nevis. He's got a lot of sleep to catch up on."

"I see."

Gladys turned to look back in Milo's direction. "Thankfully, he was able to get comfortable and doze off. Hopefully, he can stay asleep." Damien simply nodded in return. He was glad they were doing reasonably well and that others were looking out for them.

The fire continued to burn strongly through the evening. People continued to talk and converse while one by one others slowly drifted off to sleep. Rufus had taken his instructions from Damien seriously, and he had been working hard to make sure everyone was well cared for and as comfortable as they could be. Amongst all of Rufus' crazy escapades in life, it was times like this that Damien remembered why they had hired him as their lawyer. His hard work and his genuine care for people were coming out strongly.

Damien saw him approaching the fire. He called out, "Rufus!" and stood to his feet to meet him. "How is everybody?"

"They're fine. I just got done checking on Henry."

"How is he?"

"He's..." Rufus hesitated. "He's in pain." Damien looked toward the boat and took a deep breath. He didn't know what to say. He felt terrible for his friend.

Rufus continued, "Elizabeth is doing the best she can, but he definitely has a fever."

"Was he able to get any more sleep?"

"No," Rufus said, shaking his head. "Not since around noon. The pain is too strong. Elizabeth was able to collect almost all of the painkillers everyone had. But even still she figured she ought to lessen the dosage in case we're here for an extended amount of time."

Damien closed his eyes tightly. He couldn't bear this thought of his friend in extended pain and not being fully cared for as he needed to be. Henry was one of the closest friends he'd ever had. It hurt Damien to know what he was going through. He felt as if this information was more than he could bear. He needed to step away.

He began to walk away. "Well, be sure he gets plenty of water, and make sure Elizabeth has everything she needs."

"Ok," Rufus said, slightly puzzled as Damien began to walk away.

Damien walked the opposite direction from the fires into the dark of night. He wasn't going far. He just felt as if he needed to clear his head. Hearing this update on Henry brought a flood of emotions. A voice in his head started telling him that he was responsible for all this—the pain, the suffering, their current status. He tried to suppress the thoughts. If only he hadn't been so anxious to get this deal with *Worldwide Pathways*, none of this would have happened. There was a handful of reasons why this meeting shouldn't have taken place. He had just lost his daughter. His wife was in the hospital and needed to be cared for emotionally. And also, Henry had been hesitant from the beginning concerning this deal. If it was up to him, he would have probably preferred to slow things down and think through everything. There was no question he would have waited.

Damien rubbed the back of his head as all these thoughts flooded his mind. "Come on, Damien, get ahold of yourself," he said to himself. He couldn't deal with these thoughts; they made him angry and anxious. Out of habit, he looked down at his watch, but this made him even more unsettled. It reminded him of the pain and loss in his life, the loss of Lucy. He didn't need this, not now. Maybe never.

Sean was watching the detainee while Ron was helping to cook the fish. Sean wasn't as comfortable holding the gun, but he knew he could watch over him for a little while until Ron came back. Overall, he knew that, between the ropes and the fishing line, this criminal wasn't escaping anytime soon. Throughout the day, the criminal's behavior had varied from being subdued to screaming out in profanity and paranoia.

As the dark of night had come on them, the criminal particularly seemed to become more vile and filled with anxiety. Currently, he was screaming out insults to Sean. "You stupid idiots. How could you have let all of us get here? Half a sense could have told you it's not worth risking being lost in the fog. All of you should've got that captain to turn around the blasted boat."

Sean didn't respond. He had been with this man most of the day and was working hard at tuning him out. He just simply held the gun tight as he waited for Ron to return.

"That's my gun anyway! I bet you don't even know how to use that thing," the man said.

Sean turned and spoke to him very directly. "I'd watch what you say, since you are depending on us for your food and water." The words food and water were annunciated clearly. The criminal wasn't intimidated but kept on with the insults. This time he even mentioned Sean's Asian heritage as a point of insult.

It was more than Sean could take. He knew that he had better walk away from this one. As he started to step aside the criminal called out, changing his tone. "Look, hey! I'm sorry! Please... don't go."

Sean stopped for a moment and turned to look at him. He found this man's change to be puzzling. The criminal continued speaking, wiggling his body a little closer to Sean, "I... I... I'm sorry. Just please stay close."

Sean stepped back closer. "Why should I stay, especially after everything you've been saying to me? Maybe more than anything you need some time alone."

"No! No!" the man said, wide-eyed. "Please, no, not here, please don't leave me alone here."

Sean was even more intrigued. "Not here? You sound like you know where we are."

The criminal didn't say a word, but just laid there, breathing deeply. Sean was growing impatient. "Well, have you been here before?"

"No, no, I have...haven't, but I've heard of this place," he said with great paranoia in his voice.

"What are you talking about?"

The criminal slowly turned onto his back. There was great sincerity in his eyes. "There's a legend of this place in the Caribbean, an unknown mysterious island."

Sean was caught off guard. It sounded a little too fanciful. "Ok... it sounds like an old pirate story."

"No... no! It's true."

Sean didn't know if he should keep pursuing this or not. "Listen, I just spent a week with my father-in-law on St. Kitts and Nevis. I've never heard anything like this, and even leading up to the trip I did some research on the area and this story never came up."

There was a hesitant smile on the man's face. "Oh no. Oh no. You would have never heard about it. It's only the group I work with. It is a place of evil that needs to stay hidden."

Sean scratched the top of his head as he thought about what this man was saying. He didn't know what to think or say, or if he should even be listening to this man. A part of him wanted to walk away, but in the end his curiosity got the best of him. "Well, what's wrong with this supposed island? What makes it evil?"

The man kept scooting closer to Sean. There was still great sincerity in his voice. It was almost to the point where Sean thought the man was going to start crying. The man continued, looking directly at Sean. "No one really knows for sure the specifics, but they say that the Shadow of Death hangs over it. It eats away at your soul and tortures you."

Sean took a step back as he found this quite disturbing. A flood of questions entered his mind. He looked up and saw Ron walking back toward him. This was something he would need to hear.

Chapter 12

Damien and Beck hiked through the thick vegetation of the forest. It was early in the morning the next day, and the temperature was in the mid-seventies. Most likely it would get much warmer. Damien was still wearing his slacks but was down to his undershirt. Beck, on the other hand, wore cargo shorts and a tank top. Damien was one of the few passengers that didn't have his luggage with him on the ferry. Clothing options would be limited for him, but thankfully others were well supplied with various clothing items that could be shared among the group.

Currently, the two men were ascending the side of the mountain. They had taken a few minutes that morning to assess their plan and route their course before ascending. The journey was difficult since there was no trail and the foliage was thick. A couple of times, the men were cut by a branch or a passing thorn. They had found a small trickle of water coming from above and had decided to follow it, hoping it would lead to more water. Damien and Beck brought with them two large empty water bottles that a couple of passengers had given to them before their journey. The hope was that if they did find a good water source, then they could make a subsequent trip with more bottles.

"Do you think this will really lead to more water?" Beck asked as they ascended through the forest.

Damien didn't break his focus as he fought through the vegetation. "I don't know, hopefully so."

"What if we don't find any water?"

"Let's not even think about that. Let's just keep looking."

Beck smiled. "I hear ya, man, enjoy the ride. The journey is what it's all about."

Damien didn't know how to respond to that last statement. He was all for not panicking, but he wasn't sure he was ready to *enjoy the ride*. The mission was in front of him and that was to find water and possibly scope out the area. So far, they hadn't seen much, other than thick vegetation and a few birds. The hope was that the more they ascended, the stronger the water flow would become.

They hiked on for a few more minutes in silence before Beck spoke up. "So, Damien, what's your story, man?"

"What do you mean?" he said without breaking his stride.

"I mean tell me about yourself, dude. You look like you're in great shape, like maybe you used to play football or something like that."

Damien chuckled to himself as he continued to climb. "Served four years in the Marines," he said, looking over his shoulder. "Since then I've just tried to stay in shape and be as healthy as I can."

"Cool, man. You ever been in war or anything like that?"

"I did a tour in Iraq. I wouldn't say I've been in war, but I did have a couple of strenuous missions."

"Whoa, man… we got time. Care to talk about them?"

"No, not really," Damien said without hesitation.

Beck laughed slightly as he continued to climb. He decided to change the subject. "All right. Do you have a wife or a girlfriend… or maybe you roll differently?"

Damien stopped where he was and took a deep breath. He figured since Beck was helping him and would be with him most of the day that he ought to answer his questions. He turned to face him. "I have a wife named Julia. We've been married for about ten years."

Beck caught up to Damien. "Any kids?"

This question hit Damien hard. He froze. He didn't know how to answer exactly. He looked down at the ground and bit his lip. This was the first time anyone had ever asked him anything like this since Lucy passed. On the one hand he wanted to say 'yes,' knowing the memory of his daughter was vivid, but on the other hand, she wasn't here, and he thought he ought to say no. He was caught in a quandary. "Well... I ..."

Beck was caught off guard and could see Damien was struggling. "You ok, dude? Usually that's an easy question."

He turned completely around and looked at Beck. There was an angry expression on his face. The last statement upset him. "Yes, usually that is an easy question." There was clear irritation in his voice. "But for me it's not. My wife and I just lost our little girl. She died right before she was born." He took a step closer to Beck and got in his face. "So yes, for most people that's an easy question, but for me, it's not. Satisfied?"

Beck's eyes were wide as he listened to Damien. He wasn't expecting this for an answer. He brushed his shaggy blond hair out of his eyes before speaking. "Man... I'm so sorry, dude," he spoke with great sincerity. "Oh, man, that has got to be hard. Like whoa!"

Damien didn't know how to respond. He simply nodded and looked off to the side of the woods. A part of him appreciated Beck's compassion. He felt a little bad for being so direct with him.

Beck continued, "I had this girlfriend who once had a miscarriage. She always said it was so hard. Mmm... tough stuff. Just... like don't even know what to say."

"Yeah, well... let's just keep going."

The two men continued upward on the small mountain. They had been trekking for a solid hour and a half by this time. The stream's flow was a little stronger, but still not strong enough to where they could gather water from it.

149

Their one hope was that they could hear water flowing in the distance. They decided to keep following it as it flowed at an angle, coming from a higher elevation. The two men were hoping they didn't have to travel much farther because they didn't want to walk too far on subsequent trips. Nevertheless, they pressed on.

✦✦

Elizabeth the nurse looked out to sea, trying to relax. She rubbed her eyes. She hadn't slept much the night before. Taking care of Henry, and keeping him as well as she could, consumed her. Even though the blood flow had greatly slowed, she feared that he was still losing way too much blood. It worried her. He needed a doctor. Worst case scenario, she wondered how many more days he could survive like this. She didn't even want to think about the answer to that question.

Henry was sleeping now and for that she was grateful. He had a makeshift bed that he was lying on, along with a collection of jackets, used for blankets. The elderly lady Gladys gave him a small travel pillow. It turned out to be a life-saver. Rufus had also been faithful in checking on her and Henry periodically. He made sure they were well supplied with all the food and water they needed. He even took a few short shifts of watching Henry so Elizabeth could visit with her husband and son.

Elizabeth looked toward the island. She could see the people spread out on the beach. Most were sitting in shaded areas. Ron and Sean were still fishing to the left of the boat and the criminal was by their side. One of the fires was still

150

going strong as a signal, just in case there were any boats or planes in the area. Rufus was feeding it firewood periodically. Elizabeth also caught a glimpse of her husband and son playing on the beach. It brought a smile to her face.

She wished she could be with her family, but in reality, she was glad she was on the boat and not on the island. Yesterday, the brief time she had at the meeting had brought on her strange feelings. She couldn't fully explain it, but, somehow and in some way, something was speaking to her. It was her intuition, and it was telling her that she had been here before. She knew her past experience here was negative. A part of Elizabeth wanted to seek out answers, but another part of her wanted nothing to do with this place. Even having her husband and son on the beach brought her some anxiety, but she was greatly comforted knowing that they were within her sight.

So far, she had told no one about these feelings, not even her husband. She didn't know how he would take it. Also, some of the other passengers were still a little fearful about this island and were anxious to get off. If she brought up any existential feelings, it would probably raise additional panic among everyone, and that was definitely not needed at the moment. For now, these uneasy feelings would have to be kept to herself.

Her focus was broken when she heard Henry cough. She walked toward the door of the cabin and looked through the window. He was beginning to stir and would probably need her upon waking up. She took a last look at her family on the beach before opening the door and heading inside the cabin.

୧୨

The sound of flowing water became stronger. Damien and Beck knew they were getting closer to more water. They were still following the little stream, but they figured it would connect with something larger very soon. Their journey had been over two hours so far and they were ready for it to pay off. The men were exhausted and had been out of water for the last half hour.

They passed through a couple of large bushes and could see where the stream connected with a larger stream. The larger one was around three feet in width. It was following steadily as the elevation was steep. Damien was anxious to get there and quickened his pace. "Yeah, buddy," he heard Beck say behind him as he tried to follow Damien's steps.

Arriving at the stream, they could see it was just what they'd been hoping to find. Water flowed at a constant pace, obviously still from the rainfall they had within the last few days. There were lots of rocks in the stream and the water was flowing over them, giving the water a little bit of a natural filter. It's always best to gather water over flowing rocks as opposed to stagnate water or flowing through dirt or mud.

Damien didn't wait for Beck. He simply bent down and collected a few ounces from the stream. Instantly, he tipped up the water bottle and drank it down. The water was cool and tasted wonderful. Even though it wasn't totally

152

filtered, he didn't care. It was good enough for the moment. Finishing the bottle, he sat down comfortably beside the stream. He didn't realize how tired or dehydrated he had become from the hike. It was suddenly catching up with him.

He was about to dip his bottle back in for another drink when Beck tapped him on the shoulder. "Um… Damien."

"Yes?" he said, a little surprised.

"I'd suggest we go up there," he said, pointing up higher on the mountain.

Damien turned and looked through the trees. He could see that Beck was pointing up the mountain about twenty-five yards. There was a fifteen-foot rock face from which water was flowing. The rock face was a slight overhang creating a small waterfall. It would definitely be better for collecting water. "Yes, absolutely!" he said, standing up and heading that direction. Beck followed closely behind.

Arriving at the waterfall the men sat down and collected water in their bottles. Beck was using a large 64-ounce bottle that looked as if it was used in weight lifting or exercise in general. It took him a while to fill it up. Damien, on the other hand, simply had a 32-ounce bottle. They were the biggest bottles they could find among their people. Both men relaxed by the waterfall, casually drinking their fill. They would plan to bring both water bottles back filled with water for the people. They would then need to formulate a plan for collecting more water. Even with conserving, by the evening the drinks from the machine would be gone.

Damien leaned his head back against the rock wall and closed his eyes. The last two days had been quite strenuous. He knew it wouldn't last long, but for the moment he enjoyed these few minutes just to sit and relax. The waterfall wasn't very loud, and it truly was soothing. Damien thought if he let himself, he could possibly fall asleep. He'd only slept a few hours the last night, and that was after staying up all night the night before.

After five minutes or so he opened his eyes and leaned forward. He could see Beck sipping his water and fiddling with something in his shoe. It looked like he had a rock stuck in it. Damien still felt a little bad for how he had responded to him earlier when he told him about losing Lucy. He thought he would try to soften the mood.

"So, Beck..."

"Oh, hey."

"What's your story?"

Beck chuckled a little as he cocked his head to the side. He looked right at Damien with a smile. "I don't know, dude. Just clearing my mind out here on the islands. I've been clean for a year now and want to stay that way."

"Good for you."

"Yeah, thanks."

"Where're you from? Do you have any sort of family?"

He shrugged his shoulders. "A lot of family in Southern California. My mom lives in Florida. After I get off St. Kitts, I'm thinking about staying with her for some time. She's had her own issues with alcohol, but I'm rooting for her."

"I see," Damien said, nodding his head. He was happy to hear about Beck's life going in a positive direction. "What would you do after that?"

"I don't know... in the spring I finished up my GED, so I'll probably just look for work and see what I can do."

"Ok." Damien was starting to like Beck more and more. He had appreciated his help yesterday, and now especially with this conversation, he was starting to see a whole new side of this 'wild surfer kid.' It could be a little rash, but Damien thought he'd throw out some help. "Have you ever been to North Carolina?"

"Nah, man."

"Well, listen, if you ever want a new start and happen to make it up our way, then I'd love to have you come visit. Who knows, maybe we can find something for you in our company."

Beck looked directly at Damien. He smiled and nodded. "Thanks, man. I appreciate it a lot. I'll keep that in mind for sure." Beck felt his eyes begin to water just slightly. He hadn't been offered much help in his life, and for Damien to suggest this was very gracious.

"Don't mention it, buddy. Happy to do it."

Damien then turned and looked behind him up the rock wall. He then looked to the side where the wall ended. It was getting late in the day, and he knew they would need to keep progressing so they could get back to the people. Rufus was left in charge and Damien didn't know how truly comfortable he was without him around. He turned back to Beck. "I'd say, let's go ahead and see if we can make it to the top of this mountain. I don't want to be gone from the people too long."

"Yeah... sounds like a plan!" Beck stood up, excited. He was ready for another adventure.

The men made their way to the side of the rock wall and proceeded up a steep slope. It was difficult and much steeper than what they had traveled so far in the journey. They used a lot of tree branches and roots for assistance in their continual climb. In addition to this, it was getting to be the middle of the day, and the sun was overhead, heating them up. They figured they would need to make another stop at their small waterfall before continuing back down to their camp.

After twenty minutes, the men made it past the most strenuous part of the hike and were now close to the top. They could see where the trees stopped and where the mountain would peak. "All right, we're close," Damien said as he continued walking up the mountain. He walked past where the tree line stopped and toward the middle of the island. Beck was about fifteen feet behind him.

Damien reached the top of the mountain, but what he saw greatly surprised him. He could see that indeed these mountains went all the way around the island, forming a true enclosed valley below. From what he could tell the island was like a rectangle. It was around three miles in width, and maybe four in length. But all of this wasn't what truly took his breath away. For in the middle of the island, covering the whole valley, was a thick shadow, almost like a fog. It clouded everything. Damien thought that maybe he could see a few trees on the edge, but for the most part, everything was shielded from his vision. It looked dark in the valley as this shadow was lying over it. Damien was mesmerized by the sight of it.

Beck came up and joined Damien. "What is that?" he asked upon seeing the valley.

"I... I don't know," Damien said, still stunned. The two men stood standing in silence, taking in the sight that was before them. They had never seen anything like it. There was a great sense of curiosity, but anxiety, distress, and fear were what they mostly felt. They wondered what lie at the bottom of this valley.

Beck was the first to speak. "What do you think we should do, man?"

Damien, still stunned by what was in front of him, thought for just a moment before speaking quietly. "Beck, I think we better go." That was all he could say. He now knew without a doubt that there was more to this island than what first appeared.

Chapter 13

Rufus continued to do what he could for the people. He was working hard, making sure everyone was staying as hydrated as possible and in good spirits. One fire still burned strong on the beach. He made sure it was well supplied with enough wood for fuel. Their hope was that if a plane flew close by or if a ship was nearby that they would see the fire and check it out.

Most of the folks passed their time relaxing in the shade and talking with one another. Some of the people had novels they were reading, while a few worked on crossword puzzles. One of the passengers even had a small checkers and chess set. It provided a little entertainment among them. The two kids spent an hour or more playing in the sand. There were still a couple of people in the group that were uneasy, unable to relax. Their sole focus was to be saved from the island. They weren't interested in the other passengers or anything else, for that matter.

The biggest concern among everyone was the food. Most of the snacks had been eaten, and their supply was running short. At the current rate, everything would be gone by the end of the day. Thankfully, Ron and Sean had a good morning of catching fish. So far, they were close to collecting twenty for the day. The hope was that this trend would not let up any time soon.

Currently Rufus was chatting with the senior couple, Milo and Gladys, making sure they were ok. Their spot at the edge of the woods still proved to be valuable. A couple of palm trees hung just right, shading them through all times of the day. They were still uncomfortable, but overall, the couple was still trying to make the most of their situation and were careful not to complain.

"Are you sure you two have enough water?" Rufus said, standing over them. Something about his short stature gave him a naturally pleasant rapport with people.

The senior couple was seated comfortably on a patch of grass. "Yes. Thank you. We're fine," Milo responded.

"What about the temperature? Are you too cold, or maybe too hot? I could get you another jacket if you need it. How about some more food?"

Gladys smiled and shook her head. "No... we are fine. Thank you so much for taking good care of us."

Milo then spoke up, "Rufus, why don't you sit down and talk for a while."

Rufus looked behind him. "Well, I don't know. I need to check on the others and make sure the fire doesn't go out and..."

"Oh, I'm sure everything's fine. You've been working hard all morning. Why don't you sit down and visit?"

"Umm... well," Rufus rubbed the back of his neck as he thought about this suggestion. It was true that he had been working all morning. At the moment everyone seemed well cared for, and the fire was going strong. He figured he could take a few minutes to relax. "Ok, why not," he said, giving in to their invitation.

Rufus sat down in front of them. Ironically, he was still wearing his dress shirt and tie, although the tie was loosened. Long ago he had given away his coat to the St. Kitts nurse in order to help keep Henry warm.

"Would you like a cracker?" Gladys said, holding out a packet of crackers. Hospitality was in her blood and would be exhibited anywhere, even on a deserted island.

"Sure. Thanks," Rufus responded, taking one from the package. Upon biting into it, he realized how hungry he'd become. He'd been so busy taking care of everyone else that he'd forgotten to take time for himself.

"Well, why don't you tell us about yourself, Rufus?" Milo said calmly.

He shrugged his shoulders, "I don't know, not a whole lot to tell. I'm a lawyer."

"You work with Damien and Henry, right?"

"Yeah, it's good. I like it. Challenging at times, but a good job," he said as he continued to munch on the cracker.

"Have you been working with them long?"

"About three years. I got the job not too long after law school. I was in the right place at the right time. Damien hired me, and the rest is history."

"Very good," Gladys said. "Damien seems like he would be a good man to work with."

"Yeah, he's good to me."

"How's Henry today?" Milo asked.

"Umm…" Rufus struggled with how to answer. "About the same. Thankfully, he's not getting any worse. I just feel bad for him, seeing him in such pain."

"I see," Milo said softly. There was genuine concern on his face. "Well, we've been praying for him, and will continue to do so."

Rufus took a deep breath. "All right," he simply said in response.

Milo then turned the conversation to him. "Anything we can be praying about for you?"

Rufus chuckled and looked off to the side. "I don't know. I wouldn't really consider myself a praying man."

"Well, that's ok. We can still be praying for you."

Rufus was a little uncomfortable. He hoped the conversation would change soon. "Yeah, I don't know. I'll have to think about it."

Milo simply nodded in reply. He could tell Rufus was a little uneasy. He reached forward and patted the young lawyer on the arm. "It's all right, my friend. We just want you to know we appreciate all you've done so far." He paused a moment and smiled. "I'm a Bible teacher and pastor. It's always been a part of me to care for others and particularly their spiritual needs."

"Right," Rufus responded, looking at the ground. His spiritual life wasn't something he considered much. His job, financial situation, and women were his main concerns in life.

Milo continued, "While you're here, we just want you to know if you ever want to talk or open up about anything, we're here for you, ok?"

Rufus looked up and gave them a small smile. Milo and Gladys had a soft way about them and created a strong bond with him. Even though he'd still say he was a little uncomfortable, their demeanor and friendliness softened him quite a bit. He thought he should just give them something they could pray for. "I guess…" he hesitated briefly, trying to make sure he was going to say this correctly. "If you would just pray for me that I wouldn't forget anything. Damien asked if I'd help him look after everyone and I don't want to fall short and mess up." Rufus couldn't believe he'd opened up and given someone a prayer request.

"We will definitely be praying for you, Rufus."

"Thanks," he said with a brief laugh of irony.

The couple and Rufus spent a few more minutes chatting about life and telling old stories. The time seemed to slip away as Rufus enjoyed their company and the conversation. He would've said that this was the first time he truly felt relaxed since arriving on the island. Time quickly passed, and it was a full fifteen minutes later before he thought he ought to be checking on the others.

"Well, I think I should be going. Lots of work still to do, and people to take care of." he said, standing up and brushing himself off.

"Please, remember to stop by, and do take care of yourself too, Rufus," Gladys added.

"Thanks, I'll be sure to do so."

"You're welcome any time. Let us know if there's any news about help coming or communication with anyone."

"Oh, I will. Trust me, if I hear…" Rufus didn't finish his statement because at that moment he noticed something in the woods, or better yet not something, but someone. The figure was about seventy-five yards away. At first thought he wondered if it was Damien or Beck coming back, but the short glimpse he caught told him it was a young female with light brown skin. He was familiar with all the people in this group, and wondered who this could be, or even if he mistook someone from their group.

"Excuse me," he said to Milo and Gladys as he ran off into the woods. Rufus jumped over fallen limbs and pushed aside branches as he made his way toward the person. He was trying to run as straight as he could, but often a tree or bush was in the way. It threw him off a direct route to the unknown person. "Hey! … Hey!" he called out as loud as he could as he ran. He would lose sight of the girl briefly as he ran, only to gain his sight back as he moved past a tree or another impending object. As he got closer, he could see it was a girl who looked to be around eleven or twelve years of age. He continued to call out, "Hey!"

The girl saw him coming and ran off. Rufus saw she was moving but continued to run in the direction from where he saw her. He kept crying out, hoping she would talk to him. As he ran, he wondered who she was. Everyone, so far, had assumed this island was uninhabited. For him to find someone new was truly astonishing. If his sight proved correct, if this was a young girl, then possibly she would have a family with her as well.

Rufus arrived at the spot where he'd last seen the girl and found that she was gone. He looked around in every direction. *Where could she have gone?* he thought to himself. He briefly brushed aside the sweat that beaded his forehead as he frantically looked around and listened. He heard nothing but birds chirping. No rustling, no other movement, nothing. "Could I have imagined her? Surely not. She was real. I saw her clearly," he whispered to himself. This was something he would definitely need to tell Damien about when he returned.

Rufus didn't want to give up finding her, but he knew there was nothing else he could do at the moment. He took one more look around before heading back to the beach.

Damien and Beck arrived back at the beach in the early afternoon. The sight of the valley and the shadow was still heavy on their minds. Originally their plan had been to follow the water source down toward the beach and see if they could find a lower point from which to draw water.

After finding the mysterious valley before them, they hustled back to the people to inform them about what they had seen.

The two men emerged from the woods about fifty yards from the boat. Captain Jones was stepping off the boat for a short break when he spotted them. He called out to the others. "Hey, they're back! Damien's back!"

Most of the people got up from what they were doing and congregated close to where Milo and Gladys stayed. It appeared that their spot was becoming the unofficial meeting place for the group. The two men journeyed up the beach and joined the others. They were covered in sweat and very tired.

Captain Jones was the first to speak. "Were you able to find water?"

"Yeah, we had to go a little further than we anticipated." Damien said. He then held up his large water bottle. "Does anyone need some immediately?" A few people came forward with bottles to fill. Beck also held out his water bottle and shared among the people. The situation was not yet desperate as the drink machine on the ferry still had a few bottles of water left. There were also some soda and lemonade bottles, but those definitely weren't the best for fending off dehydration.

"Any sign of a boat or a plane?" Damien asked.

"No, nothing," one of the men responded.

Elizabeth's husband was the next to speak. "Did you climb the mountain? Were you able to see most of the island?"

"We did," Damien said, while looking back at Beck. He nodded also.

"What did you see?" The group became completely quiet upon hearing this question. They all stared at Damien and Beck, anxious for what they'd say.

Damien decided just to tell them directly what they had seen. "This is going to be difficult to describe, but the mountains completely surround the island, forming a valley in the center."

"Is that where the water was?" someone asked.

"No, we found the water on this side of the mountain."

"What was in the valley?"

Damien ran his hand over his head as he thought about how to answer. He wanted to be sure he was describing it to the best of his ability. He began telling them about the shadow, and how it looked like a fog hung over the area, and how he couldn't see much that lay below. The people were very curious and stopped and asked specific questions to try to figure out exactly what it looked like. More than anything, he was honest in communicating the uneasy feeling he had when looking into that valley. Beck agreed with everything Damien was saying. The people, of course, found all of this very curious. Some of the people responded in fear, while one person cried.

One of the men whose only interest was in being rescued was the next to speak. His name was Ned. He was an overweight American business man, and his expression continuously communicated a look of being upset. "I'd say if there is a valley, we explore it. We don't want to leave any stone left unturned. Maybe there's someone that can help us down there."

"I don't know, dude," Beck said. "It's not really a place you want to take a stroll."

"Hey, pipe down," he responded. "It'll be a long time before I start taking advice from a stoned-out surfer kid."

"Whatever," Beck said, rolling his eyes.

"Listen," Damien said, holding out his hands trying to calm the situation. "Let's just stick to our plan, holding together, making sure everyone's ok, and then hopefully in the next day or two help will come."

Ned was getting more upset. "Is that really your plan? Just stick around and hope help comes? We've seen nothing so far!" Many in the group were starting to feel uncomfortable at how Ned was losing his temper.

Damien continued, "Look, we can only hope. There's plenty of water up on the mountain. Tomorrow we can send out a small team to fill our bottles. We conserve our food, and hopefully Ron and Sean can catch a few fish."

Sean interrupted, "More than a few fish. Ron keeps reeling them in today. At the rate we're going, we should have plenty tonight for supper."

"Good," Damien responded. He looked down the beach and he could see Ron fishing for everyone, being a provider. He continued, "Basically, what I'm suggesting is that we hang tight and wait. It will be tough, but we can manage for a few more days. I see no need for us right now to try to venture down into that valley. Remember, too, that

167

the St. Kitts authorities and those from America are probably looking for us."

"Agreed," Beck said emphatically.

"Hey, who let this guy be in charge anyway?" Ned said, extremely upset.

Damien pointed toward Ned. "Can you calm down a second, ok? There's no need for this. We can…"

"This is madness," Ned mumbled as he walked away from the group. Damien was about to call him back, but then realized that things would probably be a lot more peaceful with him gone.

He turned to Rufus. "How are we doing on firewood?"

"We could definitely use more, especially if we want to get three fires going again like we had last night."

"Yes, most definitely." Damien then looked back toward the group. "Ok, everyone, continue looking out for each other. If you're willing and able, please help us collect firewood for tonight. Remember to take care of yourself. Also, there's no shame in taking a break if you need it." Many nodded in return. They were thankful for Damien's leadership in the midst of everything. He looked around the group at everyone's face. He knew they probably still had questions about the valley and were a little scared, but he also saw resolve in them. They would surely be watching out for one another through it all.

"Let's do it," he said, dismissing the group. The people casually got up to leave the area. There was a little chatter among them, discussing where they'd look for wood and if they had enough water.

Damien glanced toward the boat. He was anxious to check on Henry. Hopefully Elizabeth would have good news for him today. He started walking toward the boat when Rufus stopped him. "Damien!"

"Yes?" He turned to face the young lawyer.

Rufus looked a little nervous. He spoke in a quiet voice, slightly above a whisper. "I need to talk to you."

"All right," Damien said, intrigued.

Rufus looked all around him before speaking. There was great restlessness in his voice. "I think I saw someone today. Someone in the woods."

"What? ... What are you talking about?"

"I think I saw a girl, a young girl."

Damien couldn't believe what he was hearing. "Where?"

"Just over there in the woods. Maybe two hundred feet in." Rufus pointed in the direction he had run earlier.

Damien looked over at the woods where he was pointing and then turned back to Rufus. "Come, tell me more," he said. The men then began trekking through the woods, covering nearly the same path Rufus had run a few hours before. It took the men four or five minutes to make it roughly to the spot where the girl was seen.

"She was right over here... or maybe here," Rufus said, recollecting on the incident.

Damien scratched his head and looked around. He wondered if Rufus may have imagined the girl. "Are you sure you saw someone?"

"Positive!"

"Ok," Damien responded quietly. He wasn't sure what else to ask. At this point Damien figured that Rufus most likely had seen someone from their group in this area. It was probably just someone collecting firewood or answering nature's call. Nevertheless, he couldn't think of anything else that could be done. This would have to be a mystery left unsolved. More work needed to be done elsewhere. "Well... I guess we'll have to keep our eyes open."

"Absolutely!" Rufus said without hesitation.

Damien looked around the surrounding area one last time. "All right... let's go ahead and head back."

Chapter 14

"You about ready?" Beck asked Rufus. It was early morning of the third day, and the two had taken the assignment to collect water.

"Yes, just another moment or two," Rufus said as he stuffed empty bottles into a backpack. The sun was just starting to rise, and there were only a few others awake along the beach. Both men were anxious to get going as the water supply was close to empty. A few people were starting to get headaches, and most figured it was the beginning effects of being dehydrated.

"All right, that should do it," Rufus said, zipping his backpack and throwing it over his shoulder.

Beck brushed the hair out of his eyes. "Ok, dude, I figure we should just go east into the woods to the water stream. I don't think we would need to go as high up as Damien and I did yesterday."

"Do you think the stream you guys saw ran all the way down to the beach?"

Beck scratched the back of his head. "I don't know, maybe. I don't think it was quite that strong."

"Ok, well... I'll just follow you." Rufus said.

The two men ventured in the woods. They tried not to ascend too high in elevation since they wanted to find the closest spot to the beach for fresh water. Beck was the obvious choice for this excursion as he had seen the water the day before. Damien wanted to stay behind and help take care of the people, so Rufus went instead of him. The evening had been a difficult one as the people ran out of their packed food, and the last water bottles from the drink machine were taken. It was a vivid reminder that they were stranded, and they needed help to come soon. Ron and Sean were able to catch enough fish for the group to have an adequate supper. It provided a brief bit of encouragement among the despair.

For the first forty-five minutes of the journey the two men walked in silence. Both had a lot on their minds. Beck kept thinking of the valley, while Rufus' mind was fixated on the young girl he saw in the woods. They were both thankful that the walk itself had been decently pleasant since the temperature was cooler this morning than the day before.

Beck was the first to speak up, breaking the silence. "It shouldn't be too much longer."

"You sure it would be this close? You and Damien were gone for a long time yesterday."

"Yeah, you gotta remember, me or Damien didn't know where we were going yesterday." The two men ducked under a tree that was leaning. The difficulty of not having a trail still brought a bit of a challenge, but overall, it was nothing the men couldn't handle.

Beck continued, changing the subject. "Do you really think you saw someone in the woods yesterday?"

Rufus was a little caught off guard. He chuckled a little under his breath. It was apparent that rumors had been spreading among the group. He was surprised at how fast word traveled. "I don't know. I thought I did, but," he paused a moment, "the more I think about it, I just don't know. It seems crazy."

Beck laughed. "Yeah, but I wouldn't put anything crazy past us at this point. I mean, who would've ever thought we would be stranded on a deserted island for, like, three days now?"

"Well, I don't know about you, but I'm hoping help comes before we finish up this third day." Rufus began rolling up the sleeves on his dress shirt. The temperature was gradually starting to warm up.

"I hear ya. Hopefully there's a boat waiting for us when we get back."

The two men could hear the sound of the water becoming stronger. Beck was thankful they hadn't risen much in elevation before meeting this water source. They were about a mile and a half from their beach. In fact, both men wondered by how strong the stream was moving if it possibly went all the way to their shore. Arriving at the stream, the men first stopped and filled up their bottles.

"This is nice," Rufus said. "The water looks pretty clear."

"Yeah, man, if you go further up the hill there's even a small waterfall," Beck said.

"Is that where you drew water from before?"

"Yeah, but it's close to the top, quite a journey."

Rufus turned and looked toward the interior of the island, wondering how long it would take to make that journey. His curiosity was strong. "Would you want to go up and see it again?"

"No way, dude, not unless I had to," he said without hesitation. "That place gave me a weird feeling, man. Something about that thick shadow made me want to stay far away."

"Ok," Rufus said, not wanting to push the issue further. The men each drank down a full bottle of water before filling up all the others that were in their backpacks. It would be a tough journey back carrying that much weight in water.

Upon filling up the last bottle, Rufus rose to his feet and looked toward the beach. He peered through the trees but wasn't quite able to see it. He then looked toward Beck. "What do you think about heading toward the beach and seeing how far this water runs?"

"Yeah, I was thinking the same thing myself."

The two men walked back toward the beach following the stream. Already their backpacks were proving themselves very heavy. The extra weight definitely took some getting used to. Eventually they found that the stream they were following accumulated into a fresh water pond not far from the edge of the woods. It was a beautiful sight, especially with the stream forming a small waterfall that flowed into the pond. Its width was close to twenty-five feet. Seeing the pond, Beck burst with joy. "Look at this, man! Ha!" He then turned to Rufus. "You want to jump in?"

Rufus smiled. "Sure, why not?"

"All right," Beck said, excited. He quickly pulled off his tank top and took his shoes and socks off. With reckless abandonment he ran and did a cannonball into the water. It was only six feet deep. Coming up out of the water, he yelled with excited, "Whoa, buddy!" Rufus followed suit and jumped in as well. More than anything, the first thing he noticed was that the water felt like ice. A part of it was refreshing, but the shock of the temperature took his breath away. He climbed out right away and just sat with his feet in.

Both men took their time enjoying the water. Eventually Rufus got back in, while Beck had a grand time getting out and jumping in. The cold temperature didn't seem to bother him. It was truly a pleasant experience, and for a moment, the guys were able to forget about their present state of being stranded.

They spent fifteen minutes in the water before deciding it was time to go. Getting out of the pond, the men took a moment to dry off before slipping their shoes and shirts back on. "That was definitely worth it, man." Beck stated as he tied his shoes.

"Yeah, that was fun. Good way to cool off before our hike back," Rufus added.

The men threw the backpacks over their shoulders. Beck grunted as the heavy weight of the water bottles pulled on him. He took the lead as they made their way to the edge of the woods. They wanted to be sure to stay in the grass as the soft sand of the beach would be too difficult to stroll through, and this way they could also stay in the shade of the trees.

As Beck was walking along, he soon noticed something very odd—he no longer heard any footsteps behind him. He turned around and found that his suspicions were correct. Rufus was gone. He looked back and in fact he could see that Rufus had stopped not long after they moved to the edge of the woods. He was about twenty yards away. The young surfer took his backpack off and laid it in the sand. He ran close to Rufus. He was very curious at what could've distracted him.

"Hey, what's up, man?" Beck said as he got close. Rufus didn't respond but continued looking in the opposite direction. "Aren't you coming back?" Beck asked, now standing right beside his companion.

"Look at this," Rufus said solemnly.

Beck looked in the same direction as Rufus and could see what Rufus was staring at. It was the mouth of a large cave. Water was flowing into it, making a break in the beach. The mouth of the cave was twenty feet in width and just under twenty feet in height. It was coming out of a slope that drastically ascended all the way to the top of the mountain.

There were long vines hanging down from the top of the cave which shielded most of the top half of the entrance. "What is this?" Beck mumbled.

Rufus stepped closer to the cave. Beck followed behind him. They were now about forty yards from it. The young surfer was more hesitant than his companion after seeing the valley and was a little more cautious to go venturing into strange caves on this island. Rufus proceeded forward. It was truly an interesting sight. As they got closer, they could see that on the inside was complete darkness. For Rufus, the long vines added to the mystery of what was inside. He kept moving forward.

The young lawyer walked right up to the side of the cave and stood among an area of rocks by the flowing water. He slowly peeked in. He couldn't see anything, but something in the cave was mesmerizing. It could've just been the fact that Rufus was on a mysterious island and this made him even more curious. Or he thought of the possibility that there could be something in there that could help their group. He wasn't sure, but he felt as if he couldn't resist. He felt called to enter.

As he took a step forward, Beck grabbed his arm. Rufus turned to face him. "I think we should head back, man," Beck said, with great pleading in his voice.

Rufus closed his eyes and shook himself, snapping himself out of his captivation with the cave. He spoke slowly, "Yeah… yeah… I think you're right. Let's head back."

Damien collected firewood at the edge of the woods. In the past two days, very little rain had fallen on the island. This made finding dry wood a little easier. He wanted to keep moving. He needed to keep moving. Others had helped periodically, but overall there was a feeling of discouragement sweeping over the people. Most had hoped they would've been saved by now. Thinking back to his initial speech to the people, he felt bad in saying it might just be two or three days before they were saved. At the present rate, it was starting to look like he had given the people a bit of false hope.

He thought of Julia. He wondered what she was going through at the moment. She had been through so much lately between the loss of Lucy and then her surgery. Now she was probably thinking she had lost her husband. Damien wished that some way, somehow, he could communicate with her. She had always been strong, but now more than ever she was being tested.

He threw the wood down into a pile, close to where a fire was still burning. This was their signal fire which they were sure to never let burn out. It was somewhat of a challenge to do this overnight, but thankfully between Rufus, Elizabeth's husband, and himself, they were able to keep it well supplied through the night. Only once last night had it come close to burning out. Damien took a handkerchief from his pocket and wiped the sweat from his forehead. Looking down at his water bottle, he saw he just had a few ounces left. He greatly hoped Rufus and Beck would be back soon.

Bringing down the handkerchief from his face, he saw Ron walking toward him. This made him curious since Ron had been very focused on fishing and keeping an eye on the criminal. Damien could easily tell from the few days with him that Ron was a hard worker. He was just over seventy, but still in great shape. It was obvious that he was a man of many talents and gifts.

As the fisherman got close, Damien could see there was something on his mind. "What's up, Ron?"

"Hey," he said as he walked closer. "I think there's something you need to hear."

"Ok," Damien was intrigued.

"Our criminal fellow has been talking."

"More than insults and threats, I assume."

"Yeah, he's saying some crazy stuff about this island. It's looking like he might know where we are or at least he has heard of this place." There was a great seriousness in Ron's voice.

Damien rubbed his chin as he thought about what Ron was saying. "Do you think there's any legitimacy to what he's saying?"

"Well, at first we just thought he was trying to get us stirred up, but after hearing him more... I'm not sure. I think you ought to hear him out."

"Ok, let's go," Damien said, heading toward the area where Sean and the criminal were. As they approached, Damien could see that Sean was holding the gun over him. The criminal was, of course, still tied up, but he was being given plenty of water and a bit of food. Damien wondered if

179

Ron had loosened his bonds at all since he was brought onto the beach.

Walking toward the man, Damien felt a bit of anger rising up within him, specifically because of the attack on his business partner. This man was responsible for the pain Henry was going through. Damien knew some type of punishment or trial would have to wait until they were rescued. Any anger he had would have to be stifled as valuable information would need to be gleaned from this criminal. If he knew something about this island, then the three of them would need to make the most of the situation.

Coming within a few feet of the criminal, Sean walked over to meet them. "I think he's ready to talk," Sean announced.

"Yeah, Ron filled me in a little," Damien added as he kept walking close to the criminal, still tied on the ground.

Seeing Damien approach, the man spoke up, "Looks like the big boss is finally coming out to see me."

Ignoring the man's comment, Ron spoke to Damien, "He said he would talk more if it was to you directly."

"Ok," Damien said, taking a step closer to the man. He looked directly at him. "Well, what do you want to tell me?"

The man scooted his body a little closer to where Damien stood. "I'll tell you whatever you want if you loosen my bonds."

Damien was caught off guard by the proposal. His first thought was to say, 'no way,' but upon further thought, he didn't see it as a great threat, especially with Sean standing close by with a gun. He gave in. "Fine, as long as you cooperate, and do exactly as we say."

"Certainly," he said with great excitement in his voice. "You have my word, for what it's worth."

All three found this last statement ironic, but still decided to go through with it. Damien turned to Ron and nodded, as if to say, 'go ahead and cut him loose.' Ron pulled out his fishing knife and cut the fishing line on the man's hands and his feet.

"Aww…" the criminal said as his bonds broke loose. He pulled his hands forward and rubbed his wrists. More than ever he felt the soreness and cramping in his joints. He took a few moments to roll around in the sand to get the blood flowing through his muscles.

After a solid minute Damien spoke up, "Would you like some water?"

"Sure," the criminal said, breathing heavily. Ron handed him a water bottle and the man drank it down quickly. His actions reminded the men of someone who'd just finished a marathon. He was trying hard to gain back his strength.

"Now… you ready to talk?" Damien asked. The criminal nodded as he took another drink. He continued, "First, what's your name?"

"Derrick," he said in between drinks.

"Ok, Derrick, did Lex Williamson send you after Henry and me?"

"Yes, of course," he said with a bit of sarcasm in his voice. Damien figured this was the case. "No one walks away from Mr. Williamson, especially with the kind of money he offers. He figured you were on to him." As Derrick spoke, the men could hear more of his New England accent.

"Is it true he deals with black market goods?" Damien asked.

He laughed slightly. "He deals with a lot more than that. I don't even know the extent of it. He's a man of great secrecy. He only lets you see what he wants you to see."

Ron stepped forward. "Tell us about this island."

Derrick took another drink before speaking. "There's rumors among Mr. Williamson's associates about a secret island that the Shadow of Death hangs over. It preys on your fears and haunts your past. The rumors say that it makes people crazy and tortures them."

A curious look formed on Damien's face. He wasn't buying it. "Wait, this is crazy," he said, holding up his hand to stop him.

"No... no, it's true," Derrick pleaded.

Damien thought this discussion was going downhill quickly. He wasn't sure which direction he should take this conversation. "Ok, why is it then that you guys working with Lex Williamson are the only ones who know about it?"

"Oh! We're not the only ones. You got to speak with the right people in the Caribbean. Others know about it, but they try to keep it as secret as possible. Most figure it would hurt the tourism industry if word leaked out."

"But then why do you guys know more about it than others, and how is it kept secret?"

Derrick just sat staring back at Damien. He didn't know if he should answer or not. There was a fear in him that if somehow word leaked that he shared this information that he could be killed. He rubbed his eyebrows as he thought about what he should do. He was frustrated with this dilemma he'd put himself in.

Damien was growing impatient. "Tell us! Or should we go ahead and tie the fishing line back on you?"

"All right, all right, I'll tell you," he said, holding up his hands. "There's some connection between Mr. Williamson and this island."

"What do you mean?"

Derrick slowly began to try to stand up. Ron grabbed the gun from Sean and was quick to make sure it was ready. It took the criminal a few moments because of his constant soreness. Standing completely up, he answered, "I don't know for sure, but Mr. Williamson isn't just a business man. He uses his resources to keep this island secret." Derrick then paused for a moment and took a deep breath. "And I'll tell you this too. His ties go much deeper than just business. They seem to go to something supernatural... to something evil."

Damien, Ron, and Sean just looked at one another, not sure what to say about all of this. "I need to take a break," Damien said, walking away. More than ever he hoped they would be rescued from this island soon.

Chapter 15

Julia was up late watching the evening news. Both of her parents were now staying with her. She had been kept up to date by an official from the Coast Guard regarding Damien's whereabouts. Early yesterday morning she had learned that Damien, along with Henry and Rufus, had boarded a ferry that was lost at sea during a violent storm. There were also unconfirmed reports that the vessel may have been attacked before it went missing. This was curious, but she tried not to think about it too much because it was unconfirmed.

Last night the American news media had picked up on the story, and as of today it was going strong. It became the number one trending story, especially because there was a bit of mystery involved with it concerning why the ferry didn't complete the short trip from Nevis to St. Kitts. Other family members of those missing had been interviewed. Julia had been requested for an interview a couple of times, but in the end she declined. Just having endured the loss of Lucy so recently, she thought it best to stay away from the media for now.

Her father sat beside her and rubbed her back. He spoke quietly, at a near whisper. "We'll keep praying, Darling. Hold onto hope that we'll hear some good news soon." Without saying a word, Julia reached over and grabbed her mother's hand beside her. She was very thankful for their love and support.

The newscaster moved on to the latest piece of celebrity gossip. It seemed strange going from a story that had so much bearing on her life to one that didn't matter much at all in the grand scheme of things. A part of her wondered what was going through the newscaster's mind as she switched stories. It seemed a little cold, even uncaring to the families. Julia reminded herself that it wasn't the newscaster's fault. This was her job, and she was given the stories to report. Her job was simply to report them as objectively as possible.

"I think I'm going to clear my head," Julia said as she stood from the couch.

"Ok, Sweetie," her mother quietly.

Julia began walking upstairs. She was still moving slowly from the surgery. Occasionally she would feel a little pain and it would surprise her a bit. Her health was the furthest thing on her mind. Between the loss of her child and now her husband missing, the surgery now seemed like a small trial to bear. She would need to remind herself that she was still recovering.

Reaching the top of the steps, she turned and went into Lucy's room instead of her own. She kept the lights off as she comfortably sat in the rocking chair. Julia closed her eyes and leaned her head back against the soft cushion of the rocker. She wanted to be here. For her, it was turning into a room of comfort. The loss of her child was, of course, incredibly hard to bear, and at moments she didn't know if she was going to make it. But through it all she kept praying. And in her darkest moments over the last few weeks, she would say that God had brought her a peace that passed all understanding. She couldn't fully describe it, but she knew it was real.

Now she felt the same thing in regard to Damien. He was lost at sea, nowhere to be found. She couldn't explain it, but overall that same peace was surrounding her. As her father had encouraged her, she would hold on to hope and trust that God was watching over her husband.

Damien laid by the fire with his arms crossed. The sun had set two hours ago, and it was completely dark out. He was in his undershirt, using his dress shirt as a pillow. There was not much movement around camp as most of the others were trying to sleep. Rufus was still moving about, organizing the firewood for the night, and on the other side of his fire Damien could see Beck playing chess with Elizabeth's husband. It sounded like Beck was learning how to play for the first time.

Earlier in the day, Rufus and Beck had returned with water for everyone. They both met with Damien and told him of a cave that sat close to the water source. For him it was frustrating to hear about another mystery on this island. He felt no desire to explore any of it. All he wanted to do was to get these people off the island safe and sound, and subsequently get Henry the help he needed.

A couple of hours before, Elizabeth had informed Damien that Henry's condition had declined and he had a fever that was rising steadily. There also seemed to be an infection in his wound. Damien hadn't seen his friend since yesterday. It was too hard for him to see him in that condition. He was pale and looked thinner. Henry would cough periodically and then cry out in pain from it. Whenever Damien stopped to think about him, it would bring tears to his eyes. He knew these emotions would need to held in as he had to stay strong for everyone. It was difficult.

At the moment Damien felt weary with everything and was feeling a little discouraged. His mind was solely focused on being rescued. The questioning of Derrick had given them plenty to think about, but, in the end, he didn't care to explore it any further. It sounded like the stuff of legends or myths and not something he had time for. He had enough work, trying to keep the people in good spirits and encouraged as they waited for help.

Damien looked up and saw Captain Jones approaching. He had a small flashlight in his hand. Damien could only hope that he was bringing good news. "Good evening," the captain said quietly.

"Hey," Damien said, sitting up.

Seeing the fire was a little low, the captain went and grabbed a few branches to feed the fire. Damien thought it was curious that Jones was here since he usually slept on the boat. "What brings you out tonight?" he asked.

The captain sat comfortably beside his friend. "Henry," he said solemnly. "He's having a rough night." Damien closed his eyes and shook his head. This was not what he wanted to hear at the moment. "God bless Elizabeth. That poor girl is doing all she can for him."

Damien didn't know what to say or ask. Once again, this was hard for him to hear. He decided to change the subject. "Did you see anything at all on the horizon today?"

"No... No boat, no plane... nothing." Damien nodded in return. He figured this was the case. If the captain would've seen anything at all, then everyone would be informed right away.

"Checkmate." Damien heard from across the fire.

"Aw, dude, I was getting close that time," Beck responded. "Do you think you're up for one more game?"

The St. Kitts man chuckled a little in response. "Sure, maybe one more," he said as he began placing the pieces on the board.

"Glad to see them enjoying themselves," Captain Jones said.

"Yes, it is," Damien responded. Seeing the two men sitting and playing chess was therapeutic. In the midst of all their strife and chaos, the laughter of a simple game and friendship seemed like a little bit of light. Damien couldn't help but smile slightly.

Damien was about to move closer and watch them play when Rufus came running up urgently. "Damien!" he said loudly, without regard to those sleeping.

"Yeah, what's going on?" he said, puzzled by Rufus' sudden approach.

"I can't find Ned."

"So?"

Rufus kept looking around as he spoke quickly. "I mean, he's been gone for a few hours now. Before the sun set, he said something about going to the bathroom, and then when I was tending one of the fires, I noticed he was still gone."

"Could you maybe just have missed him?"

Rufus continued to talk quickly. "Maybe, but I checked with the others and no one has seen him!"

Damien looked around the beach, but he couldn't see anyone clearly. He turned back to Rufus. "Are you sure?"

"Positive."

Damien thought back to the day before when Ned strongly suggested they explore the valley. He was strong in his opinions, and according to others, he hadn't given up the idea. It was plausible to think that he had finally gotten fed up and decided to journey into the valley on his own.

"What should we do?" Rufus said.

Damien scratched the top of his head as he thought through everything. For one thing, it was dangerous being out in the dark forest at night by himself. He would need to be brought back, yet this may risk others trying to save him. Another point was what he heard earlier from Derrick. There were a lot of potential dangers brought up in the conversation. If there was some sort of connection between Lex Williamson and this island, then there was the strong possibility that Ned could put their lives in jeopardy. That was not a risk Damien wanted to take. He felt his propensity for being a Marine take over. "We've got to go after him," he said with finality in his voice.

"Now?" Captain Jones said. He and the others around had been listening in on their conversation.

"Yes," Damien said. "There are too many questions on this island, and this is definitely not the time to be venturing into that valley."

"Yeah, I think you're right," Rufus confirmed.

Damien turned to Beck, knowing he shouldn't go alone. "Beck, I'm going to need you to come with me."

"Sure, man."

"Good, grab your water. Rufus, you stay here, watch the fires, and see if by chance Ned comes back."

"Ok, be careful, Damien."

"We will." Damien quickly put his socks and shoes back on and grabbed his water bottle. They weren't sure how to find Ned, but he knew they must try. Damien also grabbed the small flashlight Captain Jones had with him.

The two men decided to enter the woods close to where Ned usually stayed on the beach. They tried to hustle through the woods since Ned had gotten quite a head start on them. They fought through bushes and jumped over logs. Their hope was that they could catch Ned before he reached the top. He was quite overweight and by no means in any type of athletic shape. Damien wasn't even sure if he could even make it to the top.

The first fifteen minutes felt like they were looking for a needle in a haystack. There was no trail and trying to guess which route Ned had taken seemed futile. Damien even wondered if maybe Ned decided to walk along the beach around the island instead of up the mountain. It would be a much safer route than trying to do this climb during the night.

As Damien was moving quickly, Beck called out, "Damien!"

He stopped suddenly and turned. "Yeah?"

"Look at this this." Beck was about fifteen feet behind, hunched down and inspecting something in the grass.

Damien walked back down to where his new friend was. "What is it?"

"It looks like the grass has been smashed down through here, like someone was walking this way."

Shining the flashlight on the area he could see that Beck's suspicions were correct. Someone had been through this area recently. It was also as if he could see shoe marks in the tall grass. It had to be Ned. Damien shined the flashlight up the mountain and he could see that the tracks were going upwards. Now they had a route to follow. This was exactly the kind of help they needed on this expedition.

"Quick, this way," Damien said as they moved more in a diagonal route up toward the top of the mountain. They began moving even quicker now, knowing they were heading in the right direction. Hopefully they could find him before he entered into the valley.

Milo and Gladys slept comfortably under the trees. They both felt a little weak from a lack of regular meals, but overall, they were doing surprisingly well for being the most senior people in the group. They kept each other's spirits high, just like they'd always had done in life through their fifty plus years of marriage. The couple had spent the majority of their days on this island talking with others, trying to be an encouragement, and also praying. Though neither of them would say the experience was pleasant, they were happy to be together.

It was past eleven o'clock at night and both were asleep. They were sleeping so soundly that neither heard the footsteps approach them from the woods. The steps were slow and methodical, careful not to wake them. A person stepped close to where Milo slept. His water bottle was right by his side. The person's hands slowly reached down and grabbed it, being as careful as possible. There was a little rustle of a few leaves on the grass, but nothing to be startled about.

The person began to slowly back away from Milo, when a voice spoke out quietly, "Would you like mine too?"

Gladys held out her water bottle. She held it toward the young lady. It was the same girl Rufus had seen the previous day in the woods. She was around eleven or twelve years old with light brown skin and dark brown hair. Her clothes were ragged, and it was obvious that she hadn't bathed in a few days. The girl jumped back, slightly afraid, as Gladys held out the water bottle.

"Go ahead… if you wish," Gladys said softly.

The young girl inched forward hesitantly and grabbed the bottle. "Thank you," she said in a heavy accent.

Gladys wondered if the girl even spoke fluent English. "You're welcome." The girl then slowly crept backwards back into the dark of the woods. Many questions filled Gladys' mind. She wondered if there was a way she could further be a help to this girl.

"Not much longer now," Damien said as he could see the top of the mountain. The light of the moon shone through the trees. It had been a difficult journey and it had taken them over an hour and a half. Beck was about thirty feet behind. He was tired, but he knew he couldn't leave Damien alone.

The trees thinned out and Damien ran to the top of the mountain. The ominous valley lay before him again. The sight of it brought back some of the terror he'd seen earlier. He quickly glanced to his left and then to his right. At first glance he saw nothing, but then inspecting further, he saw Ned, trying to descend into the valley. He was about ten yards down, trying to methodically descend the slope.

"Ned!" Damien shouted.

Ned looked and saw Damien. His face looked surprised. He was shocked and a little scared, like a kid who'd been caught stealing. He felt paralyzed, unsure if he should keep going down or come back up.

Beck caught up and joined Damien at his side. "What is he doing?" he said with disappointment in his voice.

Damien kept calling out to him. "Ned, you've got to come back!"

Ned looked down to where he was going and then back up at Damien. Even though he looked a little scared, he still shook his head. He felt as if he was at the point of no return in regard to going into the valley.

"I'm going to have to go to him," Damien said to Beck. He went forward cautiously and began moving down the slope. Ned didn't move at all as he waited for Damien. As Damien came closer, he could see that Ned was at an eight foot drop off. He wasn't sure how he'd move down past this point. It was obvious that Ned hadn't completely thought through his whole plan.

When Damien was a few feet away he spoke out. "Ned, you can't go on like this, man. We don't know what's down there."

Ned was breathing heavily. It almost sounded like he was hyperventilating. "I just have to do it. We can't just sit around. We've got to do something."

Damien looked down. It was completely dark. He could only see a few feet past the drop off. He decided to try to reason with Ned. "Listen, if you really think there's something down there that could help, then we have to at least wait until daylight to go down there. We have no idea what we'll find at the bottom. You could get stuck with no way out."

"No, no, you're just saying that... trying to scare me."

"Ned! Come on, man, this is crazy. You've got to come back up with me now."

"I'm sorry." Ned looked as if he was about to cry. "I have to do this." He started to take a step, attempting to maneuver down the drop off.

Damien saw this was a faulty plan, and Ned wouldn't be able to successfully descend this area. "Watch out!" he yelled.

The next events happened very quickly. Ned suddenly slipped and began falling. Damien reached for him and grabbed his arm, stopping him briefly. He pulled hard, trying to steady Ned, but his efforts were to no avail. He kept falling, and Damien was brought down with him. Both men tumbled down the drop off and onto a grassy slope. Ned tried to brace himself, but heard the cracking of a bone in his wrist. Damien landed on his feet, but as he hit the slope, he fell forward and tumbled down. Both men rolled for at least fifty feet. Their bodies hit an occasional branch as they rolled. Damien tried to grab ahold of a few of the branches, but he found his efforts to be unsuccessful.

The men then came to another drop off, but fortunately this one was only four feet. Rolling down the drop off, they hit the bottom with a thud, and stopped.

Chapter 16

Damien opened his eyes. At first, he saw nothing but darkness. He figured he had blacked out for a moment. Ned was beside him, moaning. Damien sat up. He touched his neck and discovered a small cut on it. He also felt various cuts on his arms, along with his head. Thankfully, nothing felt broken, and none of his cuts seemed deep.

Looking over at Ned, he saw he was sitting up, holding his wrist. His shirt was torn and there was a streak of blood running from a cut on the top of his head. It appeared that he was crying.

"You ok?" Damien asked.

He shook his head. "My wrist... I think it's broken."

Damien stood to his feet. He was upset with Ned, but he knew that reprimanding him would do nothing at this point. He turned and looked up the hill. He couldn't see anything from this vantage point. "Well, I don't think we can get back the way we came." Ned said nothing in return but just continued to hold his wrist. Damien looked further down into the valley. He wondered how far they were from the bottom. They were on the edge of a thin forest. There were tree trunks around them that looked like pines. Not much could be seen through them. The eerie feeling of the valley felt strong and more vivid. Damien didn't like this place and was anxious to get out as quickly as possible.

"Can you walk?" Damien asked.

"I don't know," Ned said quietly, still looking down at his wrist. The men were then startled by a sound in the distance. It sounded like the creaking of metal. It was frightening to them. They tried to look through the trees but saw nothing. "What... What is that?" Ned said with wide eyes.

Damien walked over and helped Ned to his feet. "Come on. We have to get going," he said urgently.

Both men began moving slowly, stumbling along the edge of the mountain, perpendicular to the slope. Their hope was that if they kept moving along, they could find a place that wasn't as steep, and they could climb out. It would be especially difficult now with Ned unable to use one of his hands. He was also still crying and seemed to be close to panicking.

As they moved along, the forest was on their right side. There was still a slope, but it could be walked on, as long as they didn't ascend or descend. Neither man had any desire to venture deeper into the valley. Any passing thought by Ned that they might find help there was now gone. It was difficult to describe, but both men would attest that this area had an oppressive atmosphere about it. The shadow was strong. It felt like a weight bore down on them, slowing them down and bringing them great anxiety. Between the sounds and the atmosphere, the men felt the urgency to escape as quickly as they could.

"Oh, God... what is this.... this... oh, God... we're going to die..." Ned cried out as they moved along.

Damien didn't know what to say in return. He just wanted to be sure Ned stayed with him. He felt similar emotions rising within him. He knew he would need an anchor in this valley. An anchor to keep him steady. He purposely thought of Julia back home. He thought of her character, her personality, her beautiful smile. In this dark moment it almost seemed unfathomable that something so beautiful could exist in the world. More than ever, he felt extremely blessed to say she was his wife. The will to be with her and to see her again kept him moving, kept him going strong.

At first the terrain didn't change much as they walked. The forest stayed to their right, and the slope stayed steep. Eventually they were even against a side of a twenty-foot tall rock wall. It went on for about fifty yards and gradually directed them further into the valley as the rock face grew larger. Damien was thankful they hadn't come down this way when they tumbled into the valley.

The metal sound continued occasionally in the distance. The unknown of the sound messed with their minds, putting pictures in them of the most dreadful things one could conjure. Later the men would say it was the fear of the unknown that was the most terrifying.

After walking for over an hour and a half, they came to an area that was significantly less steep. "This looks promising," Damien said, trying to sound hopeful. He continued to move forward, while looking up the slope. He was trying to analyze if Ned would be able to make it up to the top. Inspecting it over, he knew they would have to keep moving forward.

The slope continued to become less steep, and eventually after another fifteen minutes they came to an area Damien thought Ned could ascend. "Let's try to go this way."

"Ok," Ned responded hesitantly.

The men began to ascend when Damien stopped suddenly. He turned and looked toward the valley. Both men had clearly heard another sound, except this time there was no mistaking that it was a voice. The voice of one crying out. They felt paralyzed—not sure what to do. The voice wasn't too far away, possibly a hundred yards or more. Ned could feel himself shaking. Thoughts of the unknown, thoughts of terror continued to stir within him.

Damien was scared. He was sweating with fear. A number of questions filled his mind. He wondered if someone was in trouble or if was this valley was playing tricks on his mind. Maybe it wasn't a voice, but just sounded like one. He was no longer sure. Frightening images flooded his mind. The unknowns were growing stronger. It was like a shadow lay over his mind, clouding his thoughts. He wanted answers. He needed answers. He couldn't see anything, but Damien began to take a few steps toward the forest, toward the voice.

At that moment Ned reached out and grabbed ahold of Damien's arm. "What are you doing?" Ned said with panic in his voice.

Damien looked back at Ned and then back toward the forest. He closed his eyes tightly for a moment, clearing his thoughts. He then opened them and looked back up toward the mountain. He spoke slowly, "Ok... yes, let's go up the mountain."

"Good," Ned said with great relief.

Both men turned from the valley and began to slowly ascend.

≈≈

Zack Smithson sat on his couch in his living room, watching the early morning news. He was a pilot in his early thirties. He had a small business of flying business clients around the country. Work had been unusually slow this last month, and this week was no different. He had a couple of appointments two weeks away, but for now he was grounded. In fact, Zack hadn't flown once this past week, and that was unusual for him.

Two years ago, Zack had a large contract with *Parker & Wheaton Marketing Services.* He had flown Damien and Henry to the west coast several times to meet with another company. Over the course of four months, he had developed a good relationship with both men. Though he was no longer servicing them, he did loosely keep in touch with them through social media.

Zack was watching the news this morning, just as he had done the last few mornings, seeing if there were any new developments about the lost ferry off the coast of St. Kitts. So far there were no new developments, just a lot of speculation. He was starting to grow frustrated with all of it. He picked up the remote and turned off the television.

Lying back on the couch, Zack rested his head and looked up at the ceiling. He wondered where the ferry could have gone. He'd flown over that area multiple times. Surely they couldn't have made it too far off course. There were other islands not far from St. Kitts, and if they had strayed, then most likely they would have found one of these other islands in the Caribbean. Zack didn't want to think the worst that maybe the boat had sunk. He couldn't think that. He knew he would need to hold onto hope. Maybe there was another solution, a simple one. Maybe the rescue teams were looking in the wrong spot.

Zack sat up on the couch. He knew he just couldn't sit any longer. He had to do something. His wife was in the kitchen preparing breakfast. He called out to her, "Kathryn, I think I need to go."

Damien and Ned saw their group in the distance. The sun was starting to rise. It had taken them most of the night to climb out of the valley and then make their way back to their beach. Ron, who was already fishing, was the first to see them since they were coming toward his side of the beach. He called out to the others, "Hey! They're back!"

Most of the people were already awake and knew that Damien and Ned had gone missing in the night. After they fell into the valley, Beck had lost sight of them and made his way back to the camp. He hadn't slept as he had stayed up waiting for Damien to return. When others had awakened that morning, he had informed them that the two men were missing. It was a wonderful sight now to see them both return.

Many in the group ran close to where Ron and Sean were situated. They could see that Damien and Ned were very dirty and disheveled from their journey. "We need some water," Damien said, out of breath. Quickly, Sean handed them both water bottles.

"Is everything ok?" Rufus asked. "Beck says you fell into the valley."

Damien took a drink of water before answering. "Yes, we did. We rolled a long way down a slope before coming to a stop where it began to plateau."

"What was down there?"

Damien just shook his head as he took another drink of water. He thought carefully about what he was going to say. "We didn't see much, but it's like a great darkness lies over that valley." He wished there was some way to more thoroughly communicate how he felt.

"We also heard voices in the valley," Ned shared. Damien wished he wouldn't have said this just yet.

All the people looked over at Damien for confirmation. Great bewilderment appeared on their faces. He took a deep breath before answering. "Yeah, we think we might have heard some sort of scream or yell in the woods in the valley. Not sure."

"Did it sound like someone was in pain? Or in trouble?" Rufus asked anxiously.

"I don't know. It's hard to say. We only heard it once."

For the next twenty minutes the people continued to ask numerous questions about the valley and what they may have potentially heard. Damien also told them about the metal creaking in the distance. The people then asked questions about the terrain and if there was any way to easily enter the valley. Damien tried his best to answer their questions. Overall, he wished there was more he could do to describe the dreadful nature of it.

"Why were you up on the mountain at night?" someone in the crowd asked. Damien took another sip of water. He didn't want to say why he was there because he knew it would bring a lot of anger against Ned.

Damien didn't have to answer because Beck spoke up, "We were up there trying to get Ned to come down."

All eyes turned to Ned, who had an angry look on his face. He felt he needed to defend himself. "Yeah... so what, we needed to find some help."

"In the middle of the night?" Rufus objected.

Ned clinched his teeth. "Well, that was the only time I could get away. You guys just want to stay around here and sit on your butts all day, instead of looking for help, and..."

"Ned, calm down." Damien said, interrupting. "We've all been working here to help each other. All of us want to be rescued, but we know we have to survive. This is day four, and we don't know when help is coming."

Ned took a few steps closer to Damien. "You know what... I said this before and I'll say it again. Who put you in charge anyway? Ever since we got here, you've been calling all the shots, like you're some sort of king. In reality, you're just some pretty business man that's probably never even had any real hardship in your life."

Damien threw his water bottle down and stepped close to Ned. Anger was rising in him quickly. "Do you remember what we just went through? I just saved your life, man. And this is how you treat me?"

Ned chuckled a little. "Saved my life? I seem to remember climbing down just fine before you tried to rescue me." He took another step closer to Damien. "Oh, and do you want to tell everyone how you were about to run off into those woods and leave me there in the valley alone. It's like you weren't even in control of yourself."

Damien couldn't contain himself any longer. He stepped forward and pushed Ned as hard as he could. Ned was caught off guard. He stumbled backwards, but while doing so, he grabbed Damien's arm and pulled off his watch as he fell to the ground. "Aww!" Ned cried out as his back hit the sand.

Damien looked down at his wrist and could see that his watch was gone. He then looked toward Ned and saw his watch in Ned's hand. Seeing the watch, he thought of his mother and the pain of losing her. He could also see the broken glass on it, and it reminded him of breaking it in the hospital when he lost Lucy. Now, he was stranded on this island, away from his wife, and wondering if he'd ever see her again. Anger, frustration, and anxiety all rose within him. He felt as if he couldn't contain himself.

"Give me back my watch!" he shouted as he lunged toward Ned. His fist was reared back, ready to strike. The next few minutes were chaotic as Rufus, Beck and Sean went to grab Damien, trying to get between him and Ned. "Give it back!" Damien kept shouting. Ned scooted himself back on the sand, away from Damien. There was terror in his eyes.

After a few moments, Damien was able to break free. He jumped on Ned and pulled back his fist. He was ready to strike, but right before he could, someone came between the two men.

"Stop it, now!" yelled Elizabeth. The whole crowd became silent when they heard the St. Kitts nurse. Damien eased up and put down his fist. He felt his nerves begin to settle as he started to regain control over his emotions. He took a step back from where Ned lay.

Elizabeth continued, "Damien, Henry has taken a turn for the worse. I fear there isn't much time."

Damien put his hand on his forehead as this information hit him like a ton of bricks. Suddenly punishing Ned for his words didn't seem like such a high priority anymore. "Take me to him," he said to her.

"Yes, of course," Elizabeth said.

Elizabeth started walking toward the boat. Damien was about to follow her, but before doing so, he turned toward Ned. Ned was a little startled, seeing Damien come close again. Bending down, Damien quickly ripped the broken watch out of his hands. Ned gave it up willingly, not wanting to fight.

As they walked away from the group, Damien glanced behind him and saw the people starting to care for Ned and his broken wrist. Damien felt sorry for letting his emotions get the best of him. He wanted to be strong for these people. They had done so well at looking out for one another. He didn't want to let them down.

Climbing onto the boat, Damien could hear Henry moaning. This, in and of itself, was almost too much for Damien to hear. Elizabeth opened the door to the cabin, and there he could see his friend lying on the ground. He was shaking and there was great discoloration in his skin. Henry's eyes were closed, and he was wincing in pain.

Damien turned away as it was too hard to see his business partner and friend in such agony. "Do you have any more pain killers?" he said to Elizabeth.

"No, we're completely out. There's basically nothing else I can do for him other than keep him hydrated."

Damien leaned his head against the wall of the cabin. He felt dizzy. He put his hands over his face, trying to steady himself. "How many more days do we have before it's too late?"

Elizabeth put her hand on his shoulder. "Damien, I'm sorry, but we don't have any more days. He needs to be rescued now."

"Ok," he simply said in return. This was not what he wanted to hear. For his own sake, he knew he had to walk away. This was just too much for him to bear.

Chapter 17

A day and a half had passed since Damien and Ned had returned from the valley. It was now the middle of day five on the island. Discouragement was at an all-time high. The people were now looking slightly thinner and any thought of making the most of their situation was over. The chess games had stopped and any recreation among the group was non-existent. The people simply did what they needed to do in order to survive. Ron and Sean kept fishing, and Beck and Rufus continued to get the water. Others worked hard at keeping the firewood stocked.

More than anything, everyone's mind was on Henry. He was fading, and it was as if during the past day and a half that the people were simply waiting around for him to die. Damien had gone and checked on him two other times, but found it too difficult. His partner was in great pain, and that was not how he wanted to remember him. There was still a small glimmer of hope that they could be rescued soon, but as it was now the fifth day on the island, the people had begun to have serious doubts that they would ever be found. It was difficult for any of them to feel optimistic at this point.

Damien sat by the fire, contemplating his life. He thought back to his days as a Marine and then his time in business. He wondered if he had charted the right course for his life. He asked himself a few times that if he was to do it all over again what would he do differently. Some things wouldn't change, like his time with Julia. But he wondered if there could have been some way to spend more time with his mother. She had left him so early in his life. What could he have done differently? He knew he would never be able to find out.

As he continued to sit and think by the fire, Damien realized that he'd better get up and distract himself. He was driving himself into despair. This wasn't the state of mind he needed to be in. He couldn't do this. He needed to do something, anything to distract himself.

Damien got up and headed to the edge of the woods and started collecting firewood. Each time he found himself going deeper into the woods since much of the area had already been picked over. The thing he was most thankful for was that it hadn't rained much since they had arrived on the island. In general, this made for finding dry firewood a lot easier.

Picking up pieces of wood, Damien soon found that this simple task was exactly what he needed to help break him out of his despair. It gave him a distraction amidst the bleak situation they were in. Most of the bigger pieces of wood were gone, but he did find enough twigs and sticks to get an armful. Turning around toward the beach, he could see that he had walked about seventy yards from the camp. He began the trek back.

As Damien was walking, his foot suddenly got caught in a hole. "Aww!" he groaned as he fell face forward, dropping the wood he was holding. He was flat on the ground. Lifting himself up a little, he cursed under his breath, frustrated by his fall. He felt his despair begin to rise again. Damien beat his fist against the ground and yelled. Taking a deep breath, he hit the ground with his fist again, then again, and again. He had had enough. "Got to get out of here... got to get off this island," he mumbled to himself. He was losing his mind out here. Standing completely back up, he began again walking back to the beach. He was done with firewood. He felt tempted to simply give in to the despair.

Damien had walked about ten yards when he realized someone was watching him. He peered closer to see who it was and discovered it was not someone from the ferry. It was a girl—a young girl with brown skin, around the age of eleven. Her clothes looked ragged. Damien knew this must be the girl Rufus had seen earlier in the woods. The girl was about twenty yards away. For a moment, the two just stood staring at one another.

It was then after a half a minute that the girl took off running. Damien knew he couldn't let her get away. He began chasing after her. "Hey! Stop!" he yelled to her. The girl kept running. She was moving parallel with the beach. Damien weaved between trees and moved around bushes trying to catch her. "Please, I just want to talk!" Damien cried out.

He was moving fast and at times he thought he'd lost track of her, but then as he kept running, he would spot her again. He was gaining on her, and in fact, gaining on her quickly. The girl recognized this and started moving toward the beach. He didn't know what he was going to do when he caught her. He did wonder who she was and where she came from, but really, his first thought was that she needed help. Maybe in some way they could help her.

After running for a couple of minutes, the girl stopped at the edge of the woods. Damien thought this was curious. He continued running at full speed. Upon getting closer, he could tell she had run to where Milo and Gladys were camped. At the present moment she was sitting beside Gladys, hugging her. The young girl appeared to be afraid of Damien, and this was the place where she felt most safe.

Reaching Milo and Gladys, Damien could hear Gladys trying to speak words of comfort to the young girl. "There, there, young one. It's all right," Gladys said, stroking the girl's hair.

Damien bent down on one knee close to the girl. The girl glanced over at him. He gave her a smile before speaking. "Hey... it's ok. We just want to help." He reached over and patted her gently on the shoulder. She flinched slightly. "It'll be all right." He stood to his feet and looked toward Milo. "I'll give her some time. Try your best to make sure she stays. I'll have Ron get her some fish."

ৎৡৢ৶

The pilot Zack parked his plane by the St. Kitts airport and turned off the engine. He'd been flying over the Caribbean, looking for his friends. So far, he had seen nothing unusual. Other rescue teams were still out looking for the lost ferry. He had spoken with a few of the pilots. Optimism was low among all of them. Most were no longer looking for a boat, but were looking for wreckage.

Zack opened the door to the plane and climbed out. He would take a break, stretch, get something to eat, and call his wife before going out for another round. He knew the men were originally taking a ferry from Nevis to St. Kitts, so he used the St. Kitts airport for a base station. This morning he had been looking for them in an area south of the islands. After this short break, he decided he would start looking to the west.

Throughout this whole search the person he thought of the most was Damien's wife, Julia. She probably had lots of questions and would want answers more than anyone. Living with the unknown was most likely a strong weight to bear in and of itself. Zack also knew about the recent loss of the baby Damien and Julia had endured. He and his wife had been through a similar situation about three years before, and personally he didn't know how Julia was now dealing with her husband's disappearance while still grieving the loss of their baby girl. More than anything he wanted to find Damien for her sake.

212

As he approached the airport, Zack glanced over his shoulder toward his small plane. He felt greatly motivated not to give up. He was determined to do whatever it took to find them.

❦

For the rest of the day the people were consumed with the new young girl at camp. She stayed near Milo and Gladys. They gave her plenty of water, and she ate two fish Ron had given her. Gladys also helped her wash her hair and found her some better clothes. Her English was very broken but enough to communicate what she wanted. She spoke Portuguese, but thankfully Captain Jones knew enough Portuguese to further communicate with her. She was beginning to feel more comfortable around everyone.

It was now late in the afternoon. Damien, Rufus, and Captain Jones were gathering together with Milo, Gladys, and the girl. There were many mysteries surrounding her. They were anxious to find out who she was, where she came from, and how she got here. Damien knew that they would need to take their time as they didn't want her to feel uncomfortable in any form or fashion.

The three men joined the others and sat down comfortably. Damien was going to take the lead in the conversation, and Jones would act as a translator. "It looks like Mrs. Gladys is taking good care of you," Damien said with a smile. Jones translated for him. The girl didn't say anything in reply, but simply nodded. She then took a drink from a nearby water bottle.

213

Damien looked toward Gladys. "Has she been speaking much?"

"Every once and a while," Gladys answered. "Just phrases, like 'thank you' or 'more please.'"

Damien then turned toward Jones. "Ask her how long she has been on this island." The captain translated, and the girl answered. Her voice was quiet but not shy or hesitant.

"She says it's been close to a year. Maybe less."

"A year!" Damien exclaimed. "Ask her how she's been surviving out here for over a year."

Jones conversed with the girl before speaking to Damien. "She says that she's only been out here on her own for about two months. On the other side of the island she found mangos and bananas to eat. When she couldn't find any more, she came to our side of the island."

A number of things about this answer fascinated Damien. The thought of fruit growing on the island was intriguing, but that was not what caught his attention. "Ask her who she was with before she was alone."

Jones translated again and listened to her answer before speaking. "She says she was with many others, brought here together as a group."

"What?" Damien was even more anxious for answers. "Ask who they were. Or better yet what happened to them?"

As the captain and the girl conversed, Rufus whispered, "Damien."

"What is it, Rufus?"

He continued to speak quietly, "Do you think there's something interesting about this girl?"

"Huh?" Damien was caught off guard. "Of course, there's something interesting about this girl. She lives on this island by herself. I don't know what you're implying."

"No, I mean, does something about her just look familiar... or I don't know..."

"Just say it, Rufus," Damien said, getting frustrated.

"Does something about her remind you of Julia?"

Damien turned and stared at Rufus. This was such a strange thing for him to hear at the moment. He was upset. "Why in the world would you say that, man? Or bring this up now?"

Rufus stuttered a little. "Well... um... just looking at her facial features. Something about her eyes especially seems to really look like her."

Damien was at a total loss for words. This was definitely not the right thing for Rufus to bring up now. But looking back at the girl, Damien began to see that what Rufus said was correct. He tried to shake the idea, but now he couldn't get it out of his mind. It was true. Something about this young girl reminded him of Julia. In fact, another thought passed through his mind. The skin tone of this girl looked as if she could be Damien and Julia's daughter. He didn't like these thoughts. He closed his eyes and hoped they would go away. He had to stay focused on what was occurring.

After speaking for a while, Jones spoke up, "The girl says there are a few others, children her age. She says they came from the middle. They came from the darkness."

Damien knew they were getting somewhere. "Ask her if her parents were with her. Or just, where are they?"

Captain Jones then began the translation process. Rufus turned again to Damien. "Don't you see it, Damien? It's almost unbelievable how much she looks like your wife. If you were to tell me that..."

Damien couldn't take it. "Rufus, shut up. What do you think you're doing by this? This isn't helping anything. You're supposed to be listening and helping me here."

"But don't you just think that it's interesting."

"No, I don't. You've got to stop with this, man."

Jones was then finished and spoke to everyone. "She says she doesn't know where her parents are. Like the others, she was taken from them."

"Who took them?" Damien asked.

Jones didn't need to translate. She had already answered this. "She says she was taken by those of the darkness."

This caught everyone off guard. Her answer was very disturbing. Damien wanted to ask what was meant by her comment, but another side of him didn't want to know. This island was proving to be a place of mystery and darkness. Especially after being in the valley, he felt himself hesitating to pursue anything further that this young girl said. Another part of Damien just wanted to walk away. Rufus' earlier comments were weighing on his mind. It brought back memories of his own daughter and the loss he and his wife had endured. He didn't want to be thinking of these things now.

"Ask her what her name is." Rufus said suddenly. Just hearing Rufus' voice upset Damien even more. It seemed like

Rufus was now trying to take over. Damien wondered if this had anything to do with the things Rufus had said earlier. Jones translated Rufus' question.

Damien stood up. "I need a break," he said as he walked away. He didn't want to hear anything else, or more importantly, he couldn't bear to hear anything else. Thoughts about Julia and Lucy were strong in his mind. He headed toward the fire, where most of the others were gathered cooking fish for the evening. He figured he would just join them and try to clear his head.

As he got close to the fire Rufus ran, catching up with him. "Damien!"

"Yes?" he said, not even stopping.

Rufus seemed a little out of breath and excited. "She answered Captain Jones' question. It's incredible. She says her mom was from America and gave her an American name. You'll never guess what it is."

This angered Damien even more. "Rufus, stop this! I don't know what you're trying to do here, but this is crazy. Stop trying to find some link between her and Julia!"

"But, listen, she…"

Damien gave him a light push as he walked away. "Just leave me alone!"

Chapter 18

Another night had passed, and it was now the morning of day six. Ron and Sean had started again catching fish. Damien had been helping them with the criminal Derrick. Every morning they'd been releasing him for twenty-five minutes so he could stretch, eat, and use the bathroom. Over the last few days he had become more complacent, and Ron had subsequently rewarded him with more time out of his bonds. This particular morning Damien had helped them with the tasks, so they could get an early start on fishing. Yesterday's catch wasn't as bountiful as days prior and the two men were anxious to make up for it today. Few complained, knowing the best efforts at fishing were being given, but still everyone said they were growing extremely hungry.

Now that the tasks with Derrick were done, Damien was going to help collect firewood. He wanted to keep his mind busy. It kept him from thinking about the bleak situation they were in... that another day had passed without rescue... another day still stuck on the island. Like the days before, there was no sign of any boats or planes. In his mind, hope was all but gone.

As Damien was walking toward the woods, he spotted Rufus walking over toward him. He hadn't spoken to him since the day before when they were meeting with the young girl. Damien was still a little frustrated with how the conversation had gone the previous day. Now, seeing Rufus, he was even more upset, thinking he was neglecting his duties. Damien spoke out as the young lawyer came close, "Rufus, why aren't you with Beck, helping to get the water?"

"I sent that one guy from Minnesota with Beck. I wanted to stay and talk with you."

Damien shook his head. "I'm not in the mood for talking. Thank you." He began walking away.

"I think you need to hear me about this girl. She said some other things I think you ought to listen to."

Damien turned to face him, clearly irritated. He spoke forcibly, "Like what, Rufus? Like that she reminds you even more of my wife? Or maybe that she looks like she could be my daughter?" He paused for a moment, taking a step closer to Rufus. "The daughter I don't have! The one I lost! The one that died!"

Others in the group heard Damien shouting and could tell an argument was transpiring. Rufus countered, "No...

that's not what I'm saying. I want you to hear what else she had to say."

"Whatever, Rufus," Damien said, walking away.

"Come on, Damien... I know you've been through a lot lately, but you're kind of acting selfish. Go talk to her."

Damien turned around abruptly. "Selfish? ... Selfish?" He stuck his index finger in Rufus' chest. "All I've done is look out for you, like I've looked out for everyone else. This whole time I've sacrificed and tried to help everyone stay alive."

Rufus pushed Damien's hand away from his chest. "Well, in case you've forgotten, without me, we would've been captured by Lex Williamson's thugs on the boat. I made the first move."

"Oh, you shut up, Rufus! Don't try to act like you're more than you are. Back home you act like a stupid kid most of the time. Henry and I have had many talks about your behavior. I'm surprised we haven't fired you by now."

Hearing Henry's name brought up made Rufus extremely angry. "Take it back, Damien... take it back."

He got right in his lawyer's face. The tension couldn't be any higher at this point. "You know what? I hope you..."

"Damien!" Captain Jones called out, interrupting. He was running close to where Damien and Rufus were arguing. They were instantly distracted from their feud.

"Yes?" Damien said anxiously.

The captain was a little out of breath as he spoke. "Elizabeth said to come get you. Henry is fading fast, and she fears he will pass in a few minutes."

This shocked Damien. He already knew that Henry's condition was bad, but deep in his heart, he always thought they would be rescued in time to save him. Even now, he didn't want to believe what Captain Jones was saying. "Ok…" Damien turned toward Rufus, and instantly any anger he felt toward him was gone. "Rufus, let's go, now."

"Definitely."

Both men ran toward the boat and climbed on. They walked toward the cabin and could see Milo was on one side, holding Henry's hand. Elizabeth was on the other, holding a cool cloth over his forehead. Henry was shaking terribly and was extremely pale. Upon entering the cabin, all three looked over at Damien and Rufus. "Hey," Elizabeth said quietly. The two men froze in that moment, taking in the situation. If there were any doubts before, it was clear now that this was the end.

"Please, come join us," Milo said softly. "Henry and I were talking together, and he is at peace." *Peace*, Damien found that word ironic. Henry's current state seemed like anything but peace.

"Damien… come close," Henry said, struggling to speak. Elizabeth stood up from her spot and Damien took her place. Damien began to feel tears well up in his eyes.

"Hello, Rufus," Henry said quietly.

"Hey," Rufus returned. It was all he was able to say in response.

Henry looked toward Damien. He was still shaking. He reached out for Damien's hand. Damien was surprised at how cold his hand felt. He continued to speak through broken speech. "It looks like... I'm about to... close this deal."

Damien closed his eyes and shook his head. "No, man... no, stay with us, Henry."

"I'm sorry... Damien... carry on... take care of these people." He paused to cough. "Please, watch over... that beautiful wife of yours. Cherish her... take care of her."

Damien nodded, tears streaming down his face. "I will."

Henry continued, "And please, my friend... don't be bitter... remember... God is with you through it all... even in the hardships... and the trials." Henry closed his eyes and leaned his head to the side.

"Henry... Henry!" Damien began to shout. "Stay with us. Stay with us!"

Henry then spoke quietly, one last time. "Milo, please... the Scriptures I asked for."

Milo nodded. He also had tears in his eyes. "Yes." Milo then opened his Bible to the 23rd Psalm. He began to read slowly, but with great conviction. "The LORD is my shepherd. I shall not want. He makes me to lie down in green pastures. He leads me beside the still waters. He restores my soul. He leads me in paths of righteousness for His name's sake." Damien had his hands over his eyes as Milo kept reading. "Yea, though I walk through the valley of the shadow of death, I will fear no evil. For you are with me, your rod and your staff, they comfort me. You prepare a table before me in the presence of my enemies; you anoint my head with oil, my cup runs over. Surely goodness and mercy shall follow me all the days of my life, and I will dwell in the house of the Lord forever."

Milo then went on to offer a short prayer for Henry as he lay there. Damien didn't hear a word of the prayer; he was overcome with grief. The words of Psalm 23 were too personal for him. They were a very vivid reminder of all the pain and loss he had endured in his life. He thought back to the loss of his mother, and then recently to the loss of Lucy. Like Julia had said before he left the hospital, it felt like a shadow was hanging over him and especially now it was too much to bear. He didn't know if he could take it any longer.

When the prayer was finished, Damien opened his eyes and looked at Henry. He was hoping that Henry's eyes would be open as well. Unfortunately, he saw otherwise. Henry's eyes were still closed, and he lay motionless. "Henry?" Damien said quietly. He rubbed his partner's shoulder, hoping to get a response. "Henry!" he said louder. Still no response. "Henry!" he shouted this time. "Henry! ... Henry!" It was apparent now that his good friend was gone. Damien couldn't hold back the emotions. He beat his fist against the deck as he continued to cry.

Rufus was also crying at this point, and speaking disjointedly. "What are we going to do? He's gone. Can we still do something? Maybe he'll be ok? I need to go... I have to do something... I... I..."

"Rufus, come here," Milo said. Rufus calmly went and sat down beside the elderly preacher. Milo put his arm around the young lawyer, as he wept loudly.

Damien stood up, trying to gather himself. "I must go," he said, wiping his tears. He walked toward the door. *Could these emotions be suppressed?* he thought to himself. *I must, I need to get back to work for the people.*

Reaching for the door handle, Milo called out to him. "Damien!" He turned toward Milo without saying a word. Milo continued, "It's ok to grieve. Commit it to God. Give it to him."

"All right," he said half-heartedly, not wanting to hear this. He opened the door further.

"And Damien," Milo spoke with great sentiment in his voice. "As Henry said... try not to let it make you bitter." Damien nodded briefly before walking out.

Watching him leave, Milo could obviously tell that Damien was struggling tremendously. His many years of pastoral ministry had given him great intuition to sense when someone was carrying more than they could bear. He whispered a short prayer. "God, please be with Damien at this time. Help him with these burdens he's carrying."

Damien sat by the edge of the woods under the shade of the trees. He was about a hundred yards away from the others. The tears continued to fall steadily. He needed some time to himself. It was as if all the grief he'd endured in his life was now boiling over. He couldn't contain it any longer. It couldn't be suppressed. There was no fight left in him for dealing with these emotions.

He thought of Henry's last words to him. He had to confront this grief and pain in his life. The shadow that was hanging over his life needed to be done away with. The words of Psalm 23 came back to his mind. The Lord was with him. He needed to trust in that, believe that.

Thinking about the words of the psalm, Damien realized that he hadn't prayed much since he arrived on the island. He opened his mouth and just let the words flow. "God, I need you... I need you now. Please, stay with me. Walk beside me. I can't deal with this. It's too hard." He paused a moment and thought about what he'd just prayed. A passing thought came to his mind that he shouldn't be praying to God about this, God was the one who took Henry and Lucy away from him. God shouldn't be sought after. He should be blamed.

Feelings of anger began to slowly rise within him. He didn't like this, but he wondered if there was any legitimacy to it. Damien rubbed his forehead as he tried to think of Henry's words of admonition to stay away from bitterness. The anger was too strong. He couldn't do it. He felt as if he would have to give in to the anger. Maybe it would motivate him, help him continue on, give him resolve to get off this island.

Feelings of anger continued to rise within him, when Damien glanced down at his wrist and saw his watch. It was still broken, but he thought back to when it was given to him. He thought about his mother in the hospital, encouraging him, telling him not to let the watch become a thing of bitterness and despair, but an object of hope. The memory reminded him of his mother's peace, even in the midst of death. Damien slid the watch off his wrist and just held it in his hands. It softened him.

He continued with his prayer, except this time it was a direct release of what he was feeling. "God, thank you for the time I had with them. Thank you for the peace my mother had when she was facing death. Thank you that I saw that same peace in Henry. He wasn't afraid to die. He was ready to dwell in your house forever. Thank you for all that he did for me in life."

Damien swallowed hard. It was time for him to deal with more of his grief. He continued, "And, God, thank you for Lucy. Thank you for the time I had with her. Thank you that Julia got to carry her for nine months. Thank you that we got to hold her, even if it was just for a short time. She is our joy." The tears kept streaming. He took a deep breath as he thought about the words he was about to say. "Please, God, watch over her for us. Make sure she knows that we love her, and that she meant the world to us." He paused briefly before finishing. "Thank you that she is now living with you forever. I pray this in your name, God, and the name of your Son, Jesus. Amen."

Opening his eyes, Damien's mind felt clearer. The watch was still in his hand. He gently laid it beside him, and with his hands he began digging a hole in front of him. The dirt was loose and moved easily. The hole didn't have to be deep, but after a minute he was down nine inches. This would be all he needed. He took the watch and laid it in the hole. Slowly, he spread dirt over it. Damien would leave it on this island. In his mind it would be a symbol, a reminder that he had faced his grief, and that any bitterness that had come about would now be buried, left on the island. He wanted to face the world as a new man.

Damien stayed by himself for another thirty minutes. He took his time praying and thinking of the many memories he had with Henry. Gratitude was the word that came to his mind through it all. Henry had first given him the job with his marketing company, and he had mentored him and trained him. And then at a young age Henry let him buy into the company and be an equal partner. Nothing but feelings of gratitude passed through his mind.

Hearing footsteps, Damien turned to see that Rufus was coming to join him. His eyes were red, and it was obvious that he had been crying. "Hey, just thought I'd come to check on you."

"Hello, Rufus," he said with a smile. Tears were still in his eyes. Damien didn't mind that he was here. He appreciated his young lawyer's concern.

Rufus was relieved to see Damien smiling back at him. "We're all kind of worried about you and know this has got to be the hardest for you."

Damien nodded. "Yeah, it's rough, but..." he paused a moment before gathering his thoughts. "Henry was a man of deep faith. I don't think he'd want us worrying about him."

"I know..." Rufus stopped as he felt the tears starting to come back. "But I'm going to miss him terribly."

"Yes, me too, Rufus. I think we're still gonna have some hard days ahead, but I think he would want us to remember the peace he had. The peace we saw there in his last few minutes of his life."

"Yeah... I know what you mean," Rufus said, looking off to the side.

The two men were silent for a few minutes. Damien was still sitting, and Rufus was standing behind him. Both continued to think about Henry and the good times they had had with him. Eventually, Damien was the next to speak. "Listen, Rufus, I'm sorry about getting upset at you earlier."

"No, no... I get it. I probably should've kept quiet and not spoken up like I did about Julia and all. I'm sorry for that."

Damien shrugged his shoulders. He appreciated the apology. "It's ok. Especially there on the beach, I know you were just trying to tell me what else the girl said."

Rufus took off his glasses and looked down at his feet. He wasn't sure what else to say. He still felt a little embarrassed by what he had said earlier to Damien. Perhaps just spending a little more time alone would do him lots of good. "Well, I guess... I'll just leave you alone for a little while. I'll let everyone know you're ok." Rufus began walking away.

"Hey, Rufus." Damien said abruptly.

"Yeah?"

When Rufus mentioned their argument on the beach, something got him thinking. It made him curious. "Earlier on the beach. You were going to tell me the girl's name... what is her name?"

Rufus couldn't help but smile slightly as he looked back at Damien and spoke clearly. "Hope... her name is Hope," Rufus said as he walked away.

Hearing the girl's name made Damien smile in return. It was very fitting for the moment. Exactly what he needed to hear.

Chapter 19

It was late in the evening, and Damien was standing by the fire, looking into it. It was a beautiful evening with the stars shining brightly. Most everyone else was still awake as Milo had led everyone in a short memorial service for Henry. There was some debate in the group as to whether they should go ahead and bury him or wait. Eventually everyone decided that it was best that Damien, being his closest friend, should decide. He concluded that they should go ahead and lay him to rest. They wrapped his body and buried him in a grave. It was dug a few dozen yards away from their camp site.

Milo had done a great job leading the people in the short service for their fellow companion. He spoke of hope. He spoke of peace. He spoke of new life, resurrection. The service brought many tears, and it was especially difficult for

Elizabeth who had cared for Henry so much over the week. She had grown to love her patient while tending to him. Later on, she would admit she found great closure through the service.

Overall, Milo's message at the service had brought a spark of hope and motivation among the people. Going through this trial together brought them closer. They were working through this obstacle like they had worked through many others this past week. The people were now conversing more than they had the last few days. A few of them were beginning to mention again the idea of being rescued. Hope was rising among the people.

As Damien gazed into the fire, he felt great relief that Henry was no longer suffering. If he was back home in North Carolina, at this point his mind would probably be racing, trying to figure out what were the next steps for *Parker & Wheaton Marketing Services*. None of that mattered to him to now. Forever in his memory Henry would be seen first as a friend, not a business partner.

Damien was struck as he heard the sound of laughter a few feet away. He turned to see Beck chatting with Gladys, laughing about something. This brought a smile to his face. Laughter had been an uncommon sound these last few days, and it was ironic that on this evening it could be heard again. Damien could see others in the group smiling while they relaxed by the fire, and to his left he could see the two kids playing chess. It was a pleasant sight.

Elizabeth walked up and joined Damien as he stared into the fire. "How are you doing?" she asked.

"Hey... I'm fine," Damien said peacefully. "Thanks for asking. How about you?"

"It was a hard day, but I'm glad he's no longer suffering." There was a bit of fatigue in Elizabeth's voice. She was feeling an emotional letdown from Henry's passing. Her lack of sleep from the past week was also catching up with her.

"Yeah," Damien said quietly. It felt a little strange to be talking with Elizabeth out on the beach. Since they'd arrived on the island, she had spent most of her time on the boat with Henry. "Listen, I don't know if I got a chance to say it, but thank you for all your care for Henry. You were great."

Elizabeth smiled. "You're welcome. Very happy to do it. I only wished that I come have done more."

"No, you went above and beyond. You did all you could."

The two stood staring at the fire. Damien continued to casually take in the scene around him of everyone relaxing and conversing. Rufus had been collecting firewood and was now getting two other fires going for the night. Though the group had already eaten an evening 'meal,' some were grilling a few more fish. Ron was also bringing over some more fish he filleted, just in case some hadn't gotten their fill. Today had been the best day for fishing. Everyone was extremely appreciative of Ron and Sean for their efforts in providing.

After a few minutes, Elizabeth spoke up again. "Damien, I want to talk to you about something."

"Ok," he said, curious.

"This island is familiar to me."

"What do you mean?"

"I'm pretty sure I was here when I was a young girl. But I was much younger than our young girl, Hope."

Damien couldn't believe what he was hearing. A flood of questions filled his mind. He didn't know what to ask first. "Here? Are... are you sure?"

"Yes, I'm sure of it," she said. "Especially after hearing you talk about the valley and the shadow that lies over it, I knew I'd been there before."

"You've been in the valley?"

"Yes," she spoke confidently. "Like the young girl, Hope, I was once a child of the darkness. It is the first memories I have of my life."

"How old were you?"

She shook her head. "I'm not exactly sure when I arrived. I was four years old when I was able to escape. Eventually I ended up on the island of St. Kitts where I was taken to a children's home."

Damien turned away from the fire and tried to gather his thoughts. These memories from Elizabeth may be the first clue to their location. He looked back at her. "Do you have any idea where we are? Where this island is located?"

"I don't. I was with three other kids when we were able to escape by boat. We drifted out to sea for a few days before we were found to the east of St. Kitts. All of us were young. The oldest among us was thirteen. We didn't have a good sense of direction and we didn't know exactly which way we had come from."

"Have you told Captain Jones this? It might help him in some way."

"No, only you so far. I had a hunch earlier about where we were, but didn't know for sure until I heard about your experience in the valley."

Damien rubbed the top of his head as he thought about Elizabeth's answers. The fire continued to burn brightly. He tried to organize his thoughts to figure out what to ask next. "Ok, Elizabeth, well, how were you able to escape?"

"Yes," she said, figuring he would ask this next. "There was a man. I don't know who he was or where he came from."

"Had you ever seen him before?"

"No, but he looked like he was on a mission. He was able to free me and three others. He snuck us out of the valley, and eventually onto a boat. We then sailed out onto the sea, unsure of our direction. Thankfully, we were found after just a couple of days."

"Why didn't the man go with you?"

Elizabeth crossed her arms as she was starting to get cold. "He said he was going back to save others. He urged us to leave and that was the last we ever saw of him."

Damien turned away from the fire, looking for Jones. "Well, Elizabeth, I'd say we go to the captain and let him know what you just told me. See if there's anything that will help him figure out our location."

"Damien," Elizabeth grabbed his arm. "There's something first I want to say to you."

"All right," he said quietly.

A few seconds of silence passed. Elizabeth thought hard about what she was about to say. She hoped Damien would receive it well. "Seeing the young girl, Hope, and knowing what I went through... I think you need to enter into the darkness and save others from it. Just like how I had a savior, it's time for you take up that role and save others."

Damien stared at Elizabeth, thinking through her suggestion. The valley greatly troubled him, especially thinking about the darkness and the shadow that hung over it. Hearing her suggestion, it was as if the oppressive feelings of that area were brought onto him. It troubled him. But he also remembered hearing the cry from the midst of the trees. He remembered being drawn to the voice, knowing that it needed help, knowing that it needed to be saved.

He nodded, knowing Elizabeth was right. "Yes... in honesty, the thought has crossed my mind as well. I know it's something I need to do."

"Good," Elizabeth said quietly.

Damien took a deep breath and rubbed his chin. He quickly thought through a plan. "Let's get everyone together here in a few minutes. I'll let them know that I'll leave early tomorrow morning for the valley. I think you should also inform everyone about what you know about this island."

"Yes, I agree."

"Ok," Damien said, still thinking. He then continued to stare into the fire. A new mission lay before him. Fear and anxiety were growing in his mind, but also determination. If there were others that needed to be saved, then he was ready to enter into the valley of the shadow.

Damien lay on the beach beside the fire looking up into the stars. It was the middle of the night. He had been dosing off and on. His mind was consumed with his mission for the next morning. Earlier in the evening he had called a meeting and let everyone know that he was going into the valley. Elizabeth also had informed the group about what she knew concerning the island. There was much discussion and a few objections were raised, but in the end, everyone knew deep down that it was a good plan. Especially if there were other children trapped in the darkness, no one could argue with Damien's plan to enter the valley.

The young girl, Hope, seemed particularly pleased with the idea of others being rescued. Captain Jones tried to get more information from her about the valley, but she really didn't want to talk about it. She also said that when she dwelt in there, her vision was clouded for much of the time. Jones could tell the topic was too hard for her to discuss, and he didn't want to press the issue.

Looking up at the stars, Damien thought everything seemed incredibly peaceful. The stars were shining out clearer than he could ever remember. He wished he knew the names of the constellations and how to recognize them. Even though he couldn't sleep, he was thankful for this quiet moment. For him it was the calm before the storm.

Rufus was awake, feeding the fires. He saw that Damien was awake and stepped close to him. "Damien."

"Hey, Rufus."

Rufus sat beside him on the sand and got right to the point. "I want to come with you tomorrow to the valley."

Damien took a deep breath and looked over at his friend. "No, I don't think that's a good idea. You haven't seen this valley yet. It's definitely a place you want to stay out of."

"Yeah, and that's why I want to go. I've heard you and Beck talk about it, and if it's truly as bad as you say it is, then I want to help get anyone else out of there that might be trapped."

"Rufus..." Damien trailed off. He didn't know what to say. Rufus seemed resolute in his decision.

"Come on, Damien, let me go with you. We've been in this together since the beginning. I want to help you."

"I don't know, man." Damien shook his head. "Who knows what's really down there?"

Rufus stood back up. "Well, I'm coming with you, and I'm going to face whatever we find with you. You've been through a lot recently in your life, and this is one thing you're not going to face alone." He began to walk away.

Once again, Damien appreciated Rufus' concern. In many regards, he couldn't believe this was the same young, wild lawyer that got on the plane with him to St. Kitts. It was like he had grown much older and wiser since they arrived. Damien was proud of him, and knew he would be an asset tomorrow in the valley. He called out to him. "Rufus!"

Rufus stopped and looked over his shoulder. "Yeah?"

A big smile was on Damien's face. "Thanks."

Rufus smiled back. "No problem, my friend."

The sun was beginning to rise. Damien and Rufus packed a couple of backpacks, each with a water bottle and a few simple supplies. They didn't want to pack too much so they could be quick on their feet. If there were sudden dangers awaiting them in the valley, then they wanted to be ready to run in an instant. They were bringing the gun. Ron said they should be fine watching Derrick without one for the day. Both Damien and Rufus hoped they wouldn't have to use it.

Besides the two kids, everyone else in their group had woken up early to see them off. They all were aware that unknown dangers faced them in that valley. No one said it, but the possibility that the two men might not return was on everyone's mind. Milo had come by to pray with them, and others stopped by to wish them luck. Even Ned came by to give them his best wishes and apologize to Damien for the fight a few days ago.

"Did you guys get enough to eat?" Sean asked. He and Ron had woken up early and cooked them breakfast.

"Yeah, we're fine," Damien responded.

Ron then spoke up. "You boys have a lot of courage going into that area. Take care of yourselves." Ron himself was tempted to join them on the mission but knew he should stay behind and help watch over the people while they were gone. He also suffered a leg injury a number of years ago that slowed down his running speed.

"Thanks, Ron," Damien said. "And, hey, I want you to know how much I appreciate all you did for us this past week. I have no idea what we would've done without you and your son-in-law."

"You're welcome... happy to do it," Ron said as he and Damien shook hands. The two men had a common bond as military vets.

Damien looked toward Rufus. "Are you ready?"

Rufus threw his backpack over his shoulder. "I believe so. As ready as I'll ever be."

Seeing that they were leaving, Beck came running up. "Hey!" He looked nervous.

"Beck, what's up?" Rufus asked.

He ran his fingers through his shaggy blond hair. "I just... I don't know, dudes, I mean... and... uh... it's kind of rough in that valley... and... it's, like..."

Damien put his hand on his shoulder and spoke gently, "It's ok. What is it?"

Beck bit his lip and stared at the ground. Over the past week he had developed a friendship with these two men. He valued them both. Through his years of drug use, he had lied and double crossed most of his friends and to this day, he was greatly lacking for friendships. He realized how valuable and treasured true friendships should be. He didn't want anything to happen to these guys. "That valley... man! I just hope everything goes all right, and you make it back."

"Hey, look at me," Damien said. Beck looked up at him. "We're going to do everything we can to rescue others and make it back safe and sound, ok?"

Beck nodded hesitantly.

Damien continued, "You're a good kid. These people are gonna be counting on you. You've got to help Ron and Captain Jones take care of these people while we're gone."

Beck was on the verge of tears. He spoke quietly and sincerely, "Yes, I will."

"All right, now come here." Damien pulled him in close for a hug. He was grateful for his new young friend. He had really stepped up and done his part while they were on this island.

After releasing him, Beck spoke with a smile, "And I guess when you come back, maybe I could have that job interview we talked about."

Damien laughed slightly. "Maybe, Beck, maybe."

"Oh, and one more thing," Beck said, reaching into his pocket.

"Yes?"

Beck held out his hand and dropped something in Damien's palm. Damien looked down and could see it was a metal Zippo lighter. Beck had used it a lot this week in helping to start the fires. "I just wanted to say too, thanks for helping me keep my cool from the beginning."

Damien thought back to the first time they had ever spoken. It was when he'd ripped a joint out of Beck's mouth on the boat. He had forgotten about that. It seemed so much longer than a week ago. "You're welcome, man." Damien smiled even bigger as he slid the lighter into his pocket. "Take care, Beck."

"Goodbye," Beck said one last time before the guys walked away.

When Damien and Rufus had walked about thirty feet from the others, they looked back over their shoulders to see their friends watching them walk away. A few waved once more, and Damien waved back in return. Looking through the group, he saw Captain Jones, Hope, Elizabeth and her family, Milo and Gladys, Beck, Ned, Ron and Sean, among all the others. He was thankful for every last one of them. They all had their unique stories, and forever they would be a part of who he was. He would never forget them.

Damien turned back and looked at the beach in front of him. It was time to venture into the valley, the valley of the shadow.

Chapter 20

"Here we are," Damien said quietly. He was looking over the valley before him. The men had gone the same route Damien and Ned used for their return trip a few days earlier. It had taken them two and a half hours to reach the spot where they now stood. Damien knew this was the spot they could climb down without great hinderance, and hopefully it would lead them close to the voice Damien had heard.

Rufus stood speechless looking into the valley. He would admit that everything Damien and Beck had said about it was true. It seemed unusually dark, and the best way to describe it was truly that a shadow lay over it. The air seemed thicker too, as if some sort of fog was in it. Instantly Rufus felt like running back to camp and staying far away from this place, but he knew that was out of the question. He thought back to Hope, and remembered there could be others in this valley who needed to be rescued. No matter what, he would have to keep moving forward.

Damien took a drink of water before speaking. "Whenever you're ready, I'd say let's start to descend. This area isn't as steep as the other parts, but we should still take our time."

"Ok," Rufus said, trying to keep his courage strong.

The men slowly began to descend into the valley. They took their time, watching their surroundings, and listening closely to any sounds around them. At times the ground was level almost like they were on a path, and at other points the area was steeper, and they needed to climb down. The temperature was generally warm, but the men could feel the temperature dropping as they descended.

Damien tried to think through everything he knew about this valley, trying to see if any of the pieces would fit together. He thought of the metal sound he heard, the girl Hope, Elizabeth's account, and Derrick's mysterious words about Lex Williamson. His hope was that somehow and, in some way, he could figure out the answers to the questions he had.

They reached the point where the ground was more level. There was still a slight slope, but basically, they had reached the valley floor. There would be no more climbing at this point. The men stopped again to take a drink of water and make sure their gun was ready. They only had four bullets, but they hoped that was four more than what was needed.

Damien looked over at Rufus and could see that he had his eyes closed and he was rubbing the bridge of his nose. "Are you ok?" Damien said quietly.

"I'm...not sure. Something about this air isn't right. I feel like it's giving me a headache."

"Yeah, I remember thinking that when I was here a few days ago. I had trouble with my breathing at times."

The men then turned and progressed through a wooded area. They didn't hear much besides the occasional chirping of a bird. Damien and Rufus tried to stay as quiet as they could as they moved through the trees. In case there was anything hostile down here, they didn't want to be found out. Eventually they began to hear the metal creaking sound in the distance. "Is that what you heard?" Rufus asked.

"Yep, that's it," Damien acknowledged. He wasn't sure what else to say. The men just kept moving forward. They didn't like the sound of it, but it did give them a direction in which to go. The noise came at irregular points. Each time it lasted around five to ten seconds. Both could tell it wasn't nearby and they still had far to go.

The men carried on cautiously for many yards, stopping periodically to check their surroundings and make sure no one was around. Eventually the metal sound stopped completely. Neither men noticed it at first, but after fifteen minutes of not hearing anything, they realized it had ceased. They wondered what they could conclude from all of this.

"Let's stop for a moment," Damien said. They'd been moving through the valley for close to forty-five minutes. He took a drink from his water bottle.

Rufus was beginning to lose himself in paranoia. The feelings of oppression brought on by the darkness and the shadow were still strong. He didn't like stopping, even for a second. "Can we keep going?" he said, with trembling in his voice.

"Yeah, just one minute," Damien said as he began to look all around them. Looking through the trees to his left, he saw an open area of land. It didn't look large, maybe about thirty feet across and approximately the same distance in length. He could see something in the middle of it, but, in general, it looked like an area where the trees had been cleared. It definitely looked out of place. "Let's check this out, Rufus," Damien said as he pointed to the cleared area. Rufus looked through the trees and saw what he was referring to. He also thought this looked peculiar.

The men started moving slowly toward the area. They hid behind trees just in case there was someone close by. As they moved closer, they could see that in the middle of the clearing was a collection of stones piled together. A torch was burning close by, and other stones had been placed at random spots.

They stopped when they were about fifty feet away. "Stay here," Damien said as he moved forward. He entered the clearing and what he found stunned him. The stones had symbols painted on them. Some looked like dragons. Others looked like some type of weapons or swords. The area smelled terrible as there were animal bones scattered abroad. An animal carcass was lying beside the stone structure. "What is this?" he whispered to himself.

When Damien reached the middle of the area, he could see the structure was a memorial. It was about four feet in height, and on top there was a stone slab on which was a foreign language. He ran his hand over it and brushed off some dirt and fallen leaves. The writing almost looked like Egyptian hieroglyphics, but the symbols looked more like letters as opposed to pictures. Damien had no idea what language it was or what it was trying to communicate. The area felt like it was supposed to be religious in nature. It was all very odd.

Damien looked up from the memorial structure and saw a grey building through the woods about fifty yards away. From what he could see, it was close to twenty-five feet tall and about a hundred feet in length. There were no windows on the side of the building, similar to a warehouse. Seeing it shocked Damien, and he wondered how it could've been built in this valley. He also wondered what was inside. He thought it might have something to do with this religious site. Damien felt he must find out and started moving toward it.

As Damien stepped to the edge of the cleared area, he heard a shout. "Stop right there!" He turned to see a man pointing a gun at him, shaking. The man looked to be in his mid-twenties. His hair was black and there were dark rings under eyes. "Put your hands up!" he yelled.

Damien was shocked to see someone else here in the valley. "All right," he said, following the man's order. He thought about the gun that was behind him, tucked into his back belt. He thought about reaching for it but knew he wouldn't be able to do that with this man pointing a gun at him.

"How did you get here?" the black-haired man said. He seemed to be panicking from seeing Damien in this area.

"I… I climbed down through the mountains," Damien said, still amazed to be speaking with someone besides Rufus.

The man took a step closer to him. He was upset. "No, how did you find this island? It's supposed to be a secret." Damien didn't say anything. He wasn't sure what to say, or how he could recount their whole story of how he arrived. "Answer me!"

"Ok… ok, I was on a ferry, and we were lost out to sea. There was nothing around until we found this island."

An expression of excitement formed on the man's face. "You're one of the people Mr. Williamson is looking for." Damien didn't respond. "Oh, he's going to be so happy I found you. What are the odds?" The man started laughing.

Damien could tell this man was unstable. He wondered if he could talk his way out of this. "Listen, man, just put down the gun. I don't want to hurt you. I just want to talk."

"No!… No! We will not talk. I'll show the others what I've done. They'll see it, and you'll tell them I caught you, and…"

The man was not able to finish because Rufus ran in from the side and tackled the man to the ground. The man dropped his gun. "Damien, grab the gun!" Damien ran forward and picked up the man's gun.

The black-haired man was able to push Rufus to the side and deliver a hard punch to his cheek bone. "Aww!" Rufus cried out in pain.

Damien quickly pointed the gun toward the man. "Stop! Put your hands up!" he said as intimidating as he could. The man gave up the fight and put his hands up. It looked like fear was now coming over him. "Tie him up, Rufus."

Rufus got up and opened his backpack. He was moving slowly as his cheek hurt and was already starting to swell. He gathered a rope out of his pack and began tying the man's hands behind him. Damien kept the gun on him. Even though he greatly didn't want to fire this weapon at this man, he wanted it to appear that he wasn't afraid to use it.

When Rufus finished, he stood the man up. "Good," Damien said. "Let's take him back to the other side of the clearing."

"Ok, let's go!" Rufus commanded the man. They led him back through the clearing. They walked close to two hundred yards from the area since they didn't want anyone seeing them. Reaching a location they thought seemed safe, Damien began tying him to a tree with a rope he had brought. They also used some fishing line to tie his legs together.

"All right, time for you to talk. Who are you?" Damien said, holding the gun close.

"I'm... I'm a nobody. I was supposed to be watching the sacred place. It's my job."

"Why were you watching it?"

"I don't think I should say," he said, trembling.

"We don't have time for this," Damien demanded. "Tell us now!"

"Don't hurt me," he said, closing his eyes.

"Then tell us!" Rufus shouted.

"It's Mr. Williamson. He wants it watched at all times. He believes in all kinds of things, and it sounds really important to him. He doesn't want anyone to mess with it or come close to it."

Damien found this all very interesting. He didn't know what avenue to pursue first. "Well... what does he believe?"

"I don't know really," he said sincerely. "Something about spirits, sacrifices, and dragons. Really weird stuff. He says this island is his, and he needs it for his beliefs. It will protect him in all he does. He calls it Shadow Island."

Damien looked over at Rufus. He could tell that his young lawyer was frightened, struggling with what this captured man was telling them. Damien saw Rufus glance at him briefly. He could see that his friend was shaking. "How are you feeling, Rufus?"

"I'm ok, just a little dizzy."

"Why don't you take a break? Have a seat for a little while."

"I think that sounds like a good idea," Rufus said as he sat down. The valley was really taking its toll on him.

Damien focused again on the man sitting against the tree. "How many others like you are in this valley?"

The man looked back at Damien oddly. Something he'd said struck a chord with him. He looked a little upset. "No, I'm not like them. They hate me. I'm a joke to them."

"What are you talking about?"

"They'll see," he said, ignoring Damien's question. "I'll show Mr. Williamson that I'm doing what he wants. That he can depend on me. They'll see... they'll see."

All of this was slightly interesting to Damien, but there were other things he wanted to know more. He asked the same question, "How many others are there?"

"Seven more."

"Where are they?"

"Probably drinking somewhere... I don't know."

This was a relief to Damien to hear that there were only seven others. When they caught this guy, he figured there would be a lot more watching various sectors of the valley. He and Rufus would still have to be careful as they journeyed around the valley. He hoped he could trust that this information concerning the number of men was correct.

Damien decided to switch directions in the conversation. "What's in the building I saw in the woods?" The man didn't respond, but just looked back stoically at Damien. "What's in there?" he said more forcibly.

"Why don't you see for yourself?" the man spat back.

Damien didn't have anything to say in response. He could tell this man was done with answering questions, and, besides, he felt as if he'd already spent enough time with him. He looked toward his companion. "Rufus, do you think you're ready to go?"

"Yeah... I think I'll be fine." Rufus had his head down, still trying to steady himself. "What should we do with this guy?"

Damien shrugged his shoulders. "I guess we just have to leave him for now. I don't think he's going anywhere anytime soon."

They approached the grey building as carefully as they could. The captured man's warning of seven others was still close to their minds. They stayed low and hid behind trees as best they could. The black-haired man had been somewhat compliant and even vowed to stay silent. It was as if the terror of this place was holding him in its grip. From his anxiety, they could tell he hadn't slept much and was completely on edge while staying here.

Getting close to the building, they could see a large metal door. It was fifteen feet tall and looked rusted and weathered. It was closed now, but by looking at the hinges, they could tell that it swung open from the left side. Damien guessed that most likely this was making the metal creaking sound they had heard through the woods. A rocky path could be seen leading up to the door.

At first Damien wondered how they were going to open the large metal door, especially with it making such loud sounds. But as they looked past it, they spotted a smaller door with a window. This would be their point of entry. He grabbed his gun, making sure it was ready.

They were still ducked low in the wooded area while Damien inspected everything one last time. He then spoke

quietly, "Let's quickly get to that door. On the count of three."
Rufus nodded, without saying a word.

"One… two… three." Damien got up and ran to the door. Rufus followed right behind him. Even though it was less than a ten second run, it felt like it took forever. Their feet kicked up rocks as they ran. Every sound seemed like an explosion as they so desperately didn't want to be seen. When they reached the door, Damien didn't hesitate to break the window in the door and reach his arm through to unlock it. He cut his hand on the glass but it wasn't enough to stop him. He swung open the door, and the two men stepped inside.

Damien reached into his bag and pulled out a small flashlight. Shining the light around the room, he could see shelves lining the room and pallets on the ground. It was a large open area, much like a warehouse. Looking closely, he saw lots of prescription drug bottles on the shelves. There were thousands upon thousands of them. On another shelf he could see all sorts of guns piled up, anything from handguns to larger rifles and shotguns. He shined the light across the room and saw fuel barrels and many other gas cans. The smell of gas had hit him strong upon entering the building. Moving the light a little more, he saw another strange sight—a collection of birds in cages. Most looked like exotic island birds, but there were a couple of bald eagles among them.

"What in the world is this?" Rufus asked.

Damien stepped closer to one of the pallets on the floor. He shined his light on it. There were boxes piled six feet high. He looked at some of the wrapping around it. A lot of the writing was in a foreign language, but there was one word he definitely recognized... ammunition. He looked toward another pallet and read the word *grenades*. "Rufus, I think we have found Lex Williamson's black-market goods."

"Yeah, I think you're right."

Continuing to shine the light around the room, Damien saw two double doors across the way. "Let's check this out."

Damien and Rufus walked toward the doors. They were both locked. Damien grabbed a gun off one of the shelves. He swung it down hard against the door handle. It began to break. He tried again. This time he had success; the handle on one of the doors broke off completely. Damien set the gun aside and threw open the doors.

He was greatly surprised. He had found what he was looking for.

Chapter 21

"God, have mercy on us!" Rufus cried out as he stepped in the room. There in front of them were six children in confinement. These were the other children Hope had spoken of, the children of the darkness.

They were enclosed in boxes that looked like large plastic dog kennels. The doors of the cages were locked, but that didn't matter to the men. They quickly got to work doing whatever they could to get the children out. Rufus ran back into the larger room and grabbed a pair of bolt cutters he had seen earlier. Damien went and grabbed a utility light. He didn't want these kids being in darkness any longer. Upon turning on the light, he got a better look at them. It looked as if their ages ranged from somewhere around six years old to late teens. There were two boys and four girls of various nationalities. The men could hear a few of them speaking but didn't recognize their languages. All were dressed in dirty, disheveled clothing and looked as if they were malnourished.

As the men worked quickly, Damien took time to speak to all of them, making sure they were calm. "It's all right. We're here to help you and get you out of here." None of the kids responded to Damien when he spoke to them, but he could tell that they didn't fear him or Rufus. It was clear to the children that these men were here to help them escape.

Rufus struggled mightily at the sight of these caged children. He was crying. Seeing these kids in this state was too much for him. Unlike Damien, his life had been mostly free of hardships. He had worked diligently at his studies in school and had a good work ethic as a lawyer, but still he had viewed his life as one big party, living for today, not caring about the sorrows of this world. Working with Damien on the island had stretched his worldview, and watching Henry die before his eyes had stretched it even more. But now, seeing these kids, completely changed him. He knew he could truly never be the same man. In that moment, he determined to never live for himself again. He would need to seek greater things in life and live for the cause of others.

After the kids were released, they began gathering around Damien in the larger storage room. They were all still a little scared, not of him or Rufus, but Lex's Williamson's men and the island. Damien quickly went and found a bit of food in the larger area. He didn't recognize the language on the packaging, but he could tell it was some type of crackers.

He passed them out and the kids ate without hesitation. All the children took their turn and used a small bathroom that wasn't far away. Damien was still cautious and tried to listen carefully for anyone coming. He didn't want to hang around too long in this building, but he also wanted make sure the kids were well cared for and that they felt comfortable with him and Rufus.

One cage stood nearby that had already been opened. One of the kids told Damien through very broken English that a girl had previously escaped. He thought of Hope. "Yes, I know," Damien said with a smile. He then took his time in communicating that he was here to do the same thing—help them escape.

Rufus approached Damien. He held his hands over his head and his face was red. It was obvious he was still struggling. He spoke with great panic in his voice. "Damien, man... what are going to do? These kids aren't strong enough to hike out the way we came. I don't think... I mean... what else can we do?"

Damien put his hand on Rufus' shoulder. "Ok, take a breath, Rufus. I'm thinking it through." Rufus nodded as he tried to slow down his breathing. Damien continued, "I wonder if there's another way out of this valley. Maybe a way that's less steep. Somehow all these black-market items had to be brought in. I wonder if there's a road coming in."

Rufus closed his eyes tightly and shook his head. "I just want to get them out of here as quickly as we can."

"Yeah, I know, me too." Damien rubbed his forehead as he continued to think.

At that moment Damien's train of thought was broken by the oldest boy in the group. He was gently tapping Damien on the shoulder. He looked eastern European, but it was apparent he had understood some of what Damien was saying. "Hey," Damien said, intrigued.

"Take the boat," he said through broken English.

"Take the boat?" Damien asked, a little confused. He wondered what the boy meant. Surely the boy must be thinking that after they left the valley, they should take a boat off the island.

"What did he say?" Rufus asked.

"He said to take the boat, but I don't know what he means. This valley is definitely locked by mountains. There's no way out." Damien began to pace slightly as he thought. His mind felt like it was racing a mile a minute, trying to think through different possibilities.

Suddenly Rufus shouted out, "Take the boat!"

"What are you talking about?"

"I mean... he's right." Rufus spoke excitedly, "He means the cave."

A puzzled look came across Damien's face. "The cave close to where you got water?"

"Yes. It's not a cave. It's a tunnel. Water was flowing through it. That's how they got all these shipments in here. There's got to be a boat close by."

"Ok... I think you're probably right. Let's try this." There was no need to further discuss the matter. This was definitely their best solution for escape. Damien and Rufus both were extremely eager to rescue these young ones from the valley. The men gave the kids just a few more minutes to gain their bearings. They also took a moment to release all the birds, and soon after that, they were all ready to depart.

≈᷉᷉᷉

Damien, Rufus, and the children crept slowly through the forest valley. Close to twenty minutes had passed since they had left the warehouse. The oldest boy was directing them. It was apparent he hadn't been on the island long and remembered the direction from which he was brought. Damien was in the front of the group. He kept his gun close, but tried to keep it out of the sight of the kids. The weapon was a precaution, but he didn't want the kids to think he was leading them into a shootout.

The forest was very dark even though it was the middle of the afternoon. The men couldn't tell if a storm was coming or if this was simply the result of the shadow hanging over the valley. Damien looked back at the kids and saw that many of them looked scared. He wished he could give them some words of encouragement, but he knew that the best thing for the moment was to be as silent as possible. Rufus was in the back helping some of the young ones keep up. It was apparent that the young lawyer genuinely cared for these kids and would do anything for them.

Moving forward, Damien found himself praying. After being closed off to God for so long, he now found the words coming easily. "I will fear no evil. I know you are with me. Your rod and your staff are comforting me. Help us now as we make it through the valley."

"Damien, there it is," Rufus whispered from the back of the group. Damien looked through the woods, and, sure enough, he could see a boat.

"Yes," said the older boy as he began to move toward it. Damien followed suit, while trying to stay in the front of the group. As they moved closer to the vessel, he especially wanted to make sure they weren't spotted or ambushed.

They came within thirty yards of the boat and Damien stopped the group. He wanted to check his surroundings thoroughly before pressing forward. The boat was about twenty feet in length. It looked like a cross between some type of shipping vessel and pontoon boat. There was no inside cab, but he could see a gas-powered motor. It looked easy enough to steer.

Damien also noticed that near the boat was another building. It was smaller than the warehouse and looked to be some type of bunk house. It was two stories in height with a few windows on the side. He had many passing thoughts about who may be in there.

"What are we waiting for?" Rufus whispered.

"Just watch," he said in return.

Almost on cue, the door opened to the house and a man walked out. He was about six feet in height and had a bottle in his hand. He walked behind the building and out of sight. The older boy tapped Damien on the shoulder. "Bad men," he said quietly. Damien figured as much. There didn't appear to be any more buildings in sight, and this was probably where Lex's men were staying. The problem was that the boat was too close to the building. He knew a diversion would have to be put in place. He knew he needed to cause some type of a distraction in order for them to escape.

"Rufus, here's the plan. I'm going to go to the other side of the building and draw the men out."

"What! Are you crazy?"

"It's the only way. I'll get them out of the house and you and the kids will be free to get on board the boat and sail through the tunnel. Do you think you could navigate it out of here?"

Rufus didn't respond. He just stood there, shocked at what Damien was suggesting. He didn't like this idea of Damien sacrificing himself and then he going on alone with the kids.

"Rufus?"

He had no other choice. This was the best way. "Yes! I... I guess."

"Great. Watch carefully, stay low, and try to make sure all the men are gone before you get on that boat. Be quick and don't be spotted. I'm going to give you this other gun just in case."

"Ok," Rufus said timidly, taking the gun from Damien.

"Take care of these kids," Damien said as he left. Rufus watched Damien as he slowly crept through the forest toward the building. There was great risk in what Damien was doing. He feared he would never see him again. "God, help him!" Rufus said.

≪❧≫

Lex Williamson's men sat around a table, playing cards and drinking. The room was dark with only one overhead light. They'd been on this island for twenty days now and they were bored. This current shipment they were watching over was supposed to have been moved by now. But delay upon delay kept them waiting. These men had been hired or brought in from a few different nations in Europe and Asia. Three of them were believers and followers of Lex's religious beliefs, while the others were simple henchmen looking to make their money through the black market.

The one man who had left briefly entered back into the room. "What took you so long?" someone asked, upset.

"Shut up! Just needed some fresh air."

"Whatever, just deal the cards." It had been a long twenty days and the men couldn't stand each other. There wasn't much else to do on the island besides play cards, drink, and occasionally fight. The only thing that kept them sane and on the job was Williamson's substantial pay.

The men were not fond of the island either. Whether they believed in Lex Williamson's cultic beliefs or not, all would say there was something odd about this island. It made most of them leery, on edge, wanting to stay inside and not venture far from their dwelling.

"That's cheating!" one of the men yelled out after spotting something wrong in the card game.

"No way, that's just how the cards fell."

"You're lyin' out of your teeth. We've already seen the ace of hearts in this hand. You're pulling them out of your sleeve."

The accused man stood to his feet. "You want to come over and check that theory?"

"It would be my pleasure." He then tried to approach the other man. Quickly the others in the group rose to their feet and got in between the two of them. Tempers flared, punches were thrown, and insults abounded. Between the eerie mysteriousness of the island, the alcohol, and the boredom, fights like this were a daily occurrence.

While the group was in the midst of the fight, shots rang out and a few of the windows shattered. All seven of the men quickly dropped to the ground. "Who fired a shot?" one of the men yelled out. One more shot was then fired as the men covered the heads. A few of the men wondered if this was an enemy of Lex Williamson that had found his island for black-market goods.

Damien began running through the woods. He had fired the shots at the high windows on the side opposite from where Rufus and the kids were hiding. He didn't want the men looking in Rufus' direction. When he was close to seventy-five yards away, he turned to watch the house. He saw the men peek out of the house, and then slowly move to the side where the bullets had shattered the windows. They all looked as if they were armed with some type of rifle or shotgun.

Damien watched seven men come from the house. He waited a minute or two to make sure no one else was coming through the door. When he was sure this was all the men, he fired his last bullet into the air. The men ducked instantly and looked in Damien's direction. He quickly threw the gun down and ran off in the opposite direction of the boat. He was no longer armed. Damien didn't turn around and look, but he hoped more than anything that the men were following him.

Rufus and the children laid flat on the ground as they saw the men move out. Damien definitely had their attention. The men were moving cautiously, but still in his direction. The plan was working. It took a little while for the men to walk completely out of sight, but nevertheless, when they were gone, Rufus decided to move. "Let's go," he said quietly.

They all tried to stay low as they made their way toward the boat. Coming up on it, they could see that it rested in a pond with a waterway lightly flowing into it. It was clear that it was completely man-made—an apparent path for the black-market goods to be moved into the interior of the island. It was an effective way for Lex to hide all he was doing. The suspicions and rumors about the supernatural aspect of the island also gave it an extra cover to be hidden. If by some chance the island was discovered, then the people would be less likely to venture into the valley.

"Quick, everybody on," Rufus said. He untied the boat and helped the younger ones climb aboard. Having very little experience with boats, he wondered how to get it started. Those questions were soon answered as the older boy who was with them got to work on starting up the motor. It started flawlessly.

When the last child was on board, Rufus jumped to the controls and started moving the boat forward. He kept looking backward, nervous about the men seeing them and coming after them. "Stay down," he told the kids, while also motioning with his hands. He didn't want any chance of them being hit by a stray bullet.

Turning back around Rufus looked ahead. They were progressing toward the dark tunnel. It looked very gloomy, but he knew it was their only way to escape. He felt as if it couldn't come soon enough.

Damien ran through the woods, occasionally looking over his shoulder. He felt a range of mixed emotions. On one hand, he hoped he could see the men coming after him and not following the kids. But then on the other hand, he knew he needed to keep enough distance between them to stay out of danger himself. He really didn't have a solid plan in mind, but at this point he just kept running.

His foot hit a log and it sent him falling face first into the grass. He felt his head get cut on a random stick. His shoulder also hit particularly hard on the ground. None of this mattered to Damien. He had to keep moving. He quickly rose to his feet and continued on, running frantically.

Damien wondered if he should head back in the direction in which he and Rufus had entered into the valley. It was probably his best option for escape, but yet if the men caught him ascending, he would be an easy target for sure. It didn't seem like a good option, but it may be his only option. He began running in the direction from which he came.

Eventually Damien arrived at the warehouse again. He entered quickly and shut the door behind him. Looking out the window he had broken earlier, he could see that no one was coming. Naturally, his first feeling was relief that his pursuers were far off, but then again, he remembered that if he did see them, it would mean that they weren't following Rufus and the children. He feared for them, and knew he would need to think of something quick.

Damien turned and looked around the room, trying to see if there was anything that could be used. There were plenty of guns and grenades. He gave it a passing thought to grab some of these, but then something else caught his eyes. It was the gasoline. There were two big barrels of it along with eight smaller containers. There were even a couple of smaller gas cans, similar to the ones he kept at home in his garage. His thought was to use this fuel to start a fire in this place. This would be a sight the men couldn't ignore. He knew he didn't have time to evaluate if this was the best plan or not, he simply kept moving.

Without caution, Damien began emptying the gasoline from the containers. For two of the barrels, he simply opened their valves and they both started emptying gas onto the floor. The barrels held fifty-five gallons, and at the pace they were flowing, Damien knew they wouldn't be done anytime soon. As gas started to flow freely around the room, he realized the danger he was dealing with. He couldn't stay long; the fumes were starting to make him lightheaded.

He then went to one of the pallets filled with grenades. Damien grabbed the knife he'd brought and quickly opened one of the boxes. He threw the wrappings and dividers between the grenades to the side. Moving in a hurry, he grabbed the first one he saw, which happened to be an incendiary grenade. During his time in the Marines, he'd had some training on the use of grenades and how to effectively launch them in time of need. His plan was to throw this one back toward the building and ignite the gasoline when he was far enough away. Given the amount of gasoline, he hoped it would quickly set the place on fire.

Damien grabbed two of the smaller gas cans and walked toward the door. The gas was beginning to leak out from under the door. He looked out the window and saw that it was still clear. The men were most likely moving slowly, given that they were fired upon earlier.

Cautiously he stepped out of the door, checking his surroundings one last time. He began to pour out the gasoline liberally in a trail leading from the door. He inched himself behind the building, still trying to stay out of sight. There was a slight elevation in the direction he was going. Damien finished out the first can when he was fifteen feet away. He then started with the other can for another fifteen feet. He left a little bit of gas in the can and set it on the end of his trail. This would be the object he would aim for. He stepped back another twenty feet and took out the grenade.

Damien took a moment to look over the grenade, making sure he remembered all his training. The grenade looked fairly standard, and it didn't appear to have any surprises. He took a deep breath. If this worked, the explosion would be quite massive, and he would need to flee quickly. It was now or never.

He was about to pull the pin when he was suddenly knocked to the ground. He dropped the grenade and from the corner of his eye, he saw it roll down back toward the building into the tall grass. "No!" he yelled.

"Ha! Victory," the man over him cried out. Damien turned his head and could see the black-haired man they had tied up was now standing over him. He held a thick branch in his hand.

Damien was dizzy but tried to stand. It was no use as the man swung the branch against his side and hit him again. He cried out in pain.

The black-haired criminal continued. "It took me a long time to escape, but I did it and now I've got you." There was a crazed look in his eyes. This capture of Damien seemed to bring him great pleasure. "I'm going to give you to Mr. Williamson myself. I'll be his favorite. You'll be used in one of his ceremonies. I'll be celebrated!" He then delivered another swing of the branch against Damien's legs.

"Please..." Damien said under his breath.

"Ha! I'm sorry, but you're mine now." The man began laughing at this new turn of events. He had worked hard at freeing himself from the bonds and now it was paying off.

The world began to blur to Damien. He turned his head to the side and could see the other men coming toward him. He knew he was trapped. He wondered how much longer he had. The man continued, "They're coming... they're all coming, but I won't let them have you. This is my victory. I was doing what Mr. Williamson wanted in protecting his altar and he will be pleased. They're not going to take you from me. They are..."

Damien didn't listen to anything else the man was saying. For a moment his mind was pleased that it looked like all the men were coming his way. This would mean Rufus and the children would probably have safe passage out of the valley. The plan was working. He could rest in peace for whatever may come from these men. The mission was complete.

His mind then went to Julia. He thought of her back at home. She was wonderful, truly a great wife. She had been strong for him when he was weak. Particularly through the loss of Lucy, she had been an anchor, holding him steady. He couldn't have asked for a better companion to share life with. She was all he could've ever wanted in a wife. Even though the situation here was bleak, he knew he must keep fighting for her. He needed to get back home.

Searching for his knife or something to help, he reached into his pocket and found the lighter Beck had given him before they had left that morning. Maybe he could still set the fire. He would have to move fast. It was worth a shot. As quickly as he could, he pulled it from his pocket and got it ignited on the first try.

"What are you doing?" the man said. He started to pull back the branch to deliver another strike when Damien turned his body and tossed the lighter toward the gasoline trail. The man quickly realized what Damien was doing. "Wait...no!"

Chapter 22

Damien ducked his head as he tried to stumble away from the burning building. His ears were ringing, and he felt as if he was in a state of shock. To say that he started a fire would be an understatement. Flawlessly the gasoline trail had lit up when he threw the lighter. In a matter of moments, the fire spread to the building where the gasoline from the barrels had saturated the floor. It quickly exploded the gas canisters inside. Unknown to Damien, there were other fuels and flammable liquids in the building that also caught fire. When the fire and heat then engulfed the grenades and other ammunitions, the building didn't have a chance. The explosion was of epic proportion.

Damien looked to his right and could see the black-haired criminal, along with Lex's other men running away. His ears were still ringing from the explosion, but he could tell the criminal was screaming out in fear as he ran. The island had been unusually dry this last week, and the fire was starting to spread to nearby trees and other plant life. There was no taming it at this point. It would continue to quickly spread. The criminals recognized this and thought fleeing was their best option.

Looking down at his feet, Damien screamed in panic. His shoes were on fire. While in the building his feet had been stepping in the gas. He dropped to his side and rubbed them against the ground, trying to stop them. It was an unsuccessful effort as parts of the tops of his shoes had been saturated. Using his feet together he began trying to kick them off. "Help... God... help!" he yelled out as he got them off. His left foot was burnt a little in the process, but he didn't have time to stop and inspect. He had to keep moving.

Damien ran behind the building and circled back around to the area where he had climbed down with Rufus. The materials in the building were still exploding, and whenever a new munition was engulfed, it would blast out with a new explosion and startle him, causing him to cry out. He had always prided himself in staying steady under pressure, but this situation was further testing him.

He ran past the area of Lex Williamson's religious site. He only gave it a passing thought as he moved through it. More than anything, it helped point him in the right direction and further focus his mind. He stepped on a stone with one of his bare feet and felt a jolt of pain run up through his leg. This didn't stop him at all. His adrenaline was going strong and quickly drowned out any discomfort he was feeling.

As he moved out of the cleared religious area, he suddenly stopped. He heard a voice. It was clear. Someone was crying out, "Hey, over here." The voice tugged at his heart. Even though the fire was spreading, he knew he couldn't leave it alone.

ஜ

Zack Smithson was flying over the blue waters of the ocean when he saw smoke rising in the distance. He quickly turned his plane in that direction. He wondered what this was. Nothing on any of his maps said there was land close by. He wondered if this may be a boat on fire. The past few days had turned up empty looking for the missing ferry. He wondered if by some chance this could be someone sending out some type of smoke signal. Even if it wasn't his friends, it might be someone that needed help.

As he approached the smoke, he realized that it came from an island. This brought a great mystery to his mind. Zack knew this area well enough to know there was not supposed to be an island in this territory. He picked up a paper map beside him and, sure enough, there didn't appear to be any island here. He kept moving forward and saw that the island wasn't huge, but it was big enough that he should have heard about it in his search.

Coming closer, he could see that the smoke was rising from the middle of the island. He found it interesting that the land contained a valley completely enclosed by mountains. Seeing the smoke coming from the top, Zack had a passing thought that this looked like some type of volcano erupting, but upon getting closer he found it was definitely an average island with a fire burning in its interior.

Zack looked out his side window and could see another small fire burning on the beach. He now could see what looked like twenty people waving at him as he passed by. He also spotted a boat close by. It was the lost ferry. Zack put his hand over his mouth in shock. He couldn't believe it, but he had found them.

He did a quick fly over the island before turning away. Authorities would need to be contacted immediately. These people had been stranded for about a week. There was no time to lose.

Damien ran toward the voice. The fire still blazed close by. With every step it felt like his feet were getting cut by a stick or something else he stepped on. His mind was still racing, trying to evaluate different scenarios, specifically where this individual was and what was the best way out of the valley. He continued to cry out to God as he ran.

After running about forty yards, he saw a small makeshift shelter and under the shelter sat a young black-haired girl. She appeared to be about ten years old. The girl was very surprised to see him. Like the others they had rescued earlier, she was dirty and facing malnutrition. She was also holding tightly to her arm. She had escaped from Lex's men earlier, and she knew instantly that Damien was not one of them.

Damien realized that this must actually be the young girl the other kids said had escaped. The Portuguese girl, Hope, had escaped months ago, probably before the other kids had come to the island. They wouldn't have known about her. This was definitely the girl they were referring to.

"Can you walk?" Damien said urgently, hoping the girl understood English.

"Yeah... but my arm... it's broken." The girl had a slight accent.

"Ok, let's go," Damien helped her to her feet. He looked out in the direction from which he had come. Unfortunately, he found that the fire had spread around it and there was no going back.

Damien looked around, frantically searching for something to help guide him. "Help me, God... help..."

"We need to go the other way," the girl said loudly, pointing to a direction further from where he came.

"Are you sure?"

"Yes," the girl said, wide-eyed. "There's a place I went to get water."

"Ok." Damien began moving through the trees in the general direction where the girl pointed. He found the girl struggling to walk quickly as she was cautiously holding her arm with every step. Damien picked her up and continued running through the trees.

"Hey, everyone... look!" Captain Jones exclaimed as Rufus came toward them on the boat. The people on the beach were shocked to see him on a boat with half a dozen children. Already they had a plethora of questions. They had gathered by the ferry when they had heard the explosion from inside the valley. Many of them were scared at first, but then their minds were completely distracted by the plane that flew overhead. There was a strange mixture of concern from the fire, joy from seeing the plane overhead, and also relief from Rufus coming toward them in a boat.

Upon seeing the boat come closer, Hope shouted out with joy. She knew these must be other kids who came from the valley... in the darkness. As Rufus parked the vessel on the shore, she couldn't be held back in climbing onto the boat and speaking to the other children. She was beyond excited that others had been saved.

Rufus cut the motor and exited the boat. The whole group was gathered around him, hungry for information. Captain Jones was the first to speak. "Rufus, what happened?"

"I'm not sure." Rufus looked up and saw the smoke coming from the interior of the island. "Damien and I found the children and we escaped through a tunnel. Just when we got out, I heard the explosion."

"Where's Damien?" Elizabeth asked.

He shook his head. "I don't know. He stayed behind and distracted a group of crooks away from us. I don't know what happened after that."

Everyone in the group stood there anxiously. Many had questions for Rufus, but at this point no one brought them up. Their minds were now filled with concern for their missing friend. A few even wondered if they should climb the mountain and see if they could spot him in the valley or find him below, but they knew the chances of finding him were a long shot.

After a few moments Rufus spoke up. He had a plan. "Let's get the children off the boat. I can then take it around and see if Damien made it out of the valley and maybe he's somewhere around the beach. If not, then I can enter back through the tunnel and hopefully there…"

Rufus was instantly distracted as Hope spoke out from the boat to the captain. He listened closely for a moment before asking a follow-up question.

"What's she saying?" Rufus asked.

Captain Jones turned to him. "She says that the other children are saying that another girl escaped and is probably still in the valley."

"Is she sure?"

"Oh, yes, the others say she escaped a few days ago."

Rufus turned from the group and paced slightly. He took his glasses off as he thought to himself. He remembered seeing the kids trapped in that valley. He couldn't bear the thought of leaving one behind. Rufus struggled greatly with this. "Oh, no… oh, no," he whispered, trying to calm himself. He got down on one knee and rubbed the bridge of his nose. He felt dizzy, thinking about the child left behind. It was a weight too heavy for him to bear.

It was then that a thought came to Rufus's mind. It was Damien. He thought of his companion still there in the valley. He didn't know how it would happen, but he felt a little glimmer of hope, knowing that somehow Damien could save this last lost girl. It felt like a long shot, but it was enough to keep him moving forward.

He walked back toward the group. "Let's help the kids get off the boat. I'm going to take it around the island for when I see Damien coming out of the valley with the girl."

Many in the group didn't know what to say. Rufus' comment caught them off guard. Some in the group nodded their heads. His hope was infectious. It was exactly what the people needed to hear in that moment.

Captain Jones put his hand on the young lawyer's shoulder and smiled. "I like your confidence, young man." He paused just a moment before continuing, "And I think I'll come with you and lend you a hand."

"Good," Rufus responded. "I think I'll need it."

❧⋆❧

Damien carried the girl through the forest. He had run for ten minutes with her in his arms. Every moment was crucial as the fire continued to spread. He began coughing as the smoke was growing stronger. The heat was also getting to him. He knew he couldn't stop moving. Both his life and the girl's life depended on it.

"Just a little further," the girl said, trying to direct him. She had been through a lot these last couple of weeks, and her resiliency had grown strong.

As Damien continued running, he realized that the fire was now on his left and his right. His fear was that it would soon enclose around him, trapping them both. He ran faster, hoping he could reach a point where he was no longer surrounded by fire on both sides. A part of him felt as if he was running in vain, knowing he wouldn't escape. He couldn't think like this. He had to continue on.

"Over there!" the girl shouted.

Damien moved forward but could see that the fire was now in front of him as well. He quickly looked behind him and saw the fire growing behind him. There was no point in turning around. Everything now looked hopeless.

Before Damien could sink any further into despair, the girl spoke out. "You've got to go through the fire!"

"What?"

"Right there," she was pointing forward to a spot twenty feet from where they stood.

"I don't see anything."

"Look closely," the girl spoke quickly. "There's a spot between those two bushes."

The fire was burning strong, but Damien did see what looked like a small path he could possibly get through. The fire would most likely still burn him, but it appeared he could make it a few feet if it cleared up on the other side. There was no telling what was on the other side but if it was more burning trees and vegetation, then it would most likely mean imminent death.

"There's got to be another way," he said to the girl.

"No! Please, you've got to hurry. We'll be ok, if we make it through... have faith."

Those last two words from the girl caught him off guard. It was strange hearing these words come from a young child. It was exactly what these last three weeks had been about—having faith, trusting in God's leading, and following the Good Shepherd. This would be one more trial he would need to face. Damien greatly feared for them both. He couldn't see the other side, but he knew there was no other option. He whispered a short prayer, "God, help me in this. Protect us as we pass through the fire."

His fear was still strong, but he found the courage to move forward. The girl buried her head into his chest and looked away. As Damien got close to the path, he closed his eyes and ran through it, holding the girl as tightly as he could. It only lasted a fraction of a second, but it felt as if his whole body was on fire from the extreme heat. Some of the skin on his hands and neck were singed as he ran through the flames.

Making it through to the other side, Damien collapsed. He grabbed the side of his neck, trying to ease the pain searing through his skin. The girl fell out of his arms, but quickly gathered herself. "Come on!" she yelled to Damien. She pulled on his arm. Damien climbed back to his feet and began moving forward.

Everything was a little bit of a blur, but he could see that they were in between two large rocks. A five-foot wide path was in front of them. They both hustled forward through the rocks. After a few feet, one of the rocks came to an end and Damien could see the small water hole the girl mentioned earlier. To his left was still a large rock face that was twelve feet high, but he saw no trees or vegetation close by, nothing that would catch fire.

Looking around, what surprised Damien the most was what he saw in front of him. It was a straight path, a trail ascending out of the valley. He looked forward and could see that it was leading them to a place on the mountains that was lower in elevation. It was between two peaks. This truly was the easiest way over the mountains he had yet seen.

"Thank you, God," Damien said as he moved forward. Even though he had to pass through the fire, the path out of the valley had been made clear.

Chapter 23

The captain drove the boat as Rufus looked out toward the beach. Rufus had suggested the captain should drive since he had a lot more experience driving a boat. Neither spoke as both were focused on finding Damien. This was their second trip around the island, and so far, they'd seen nothing out of the ordinary. They'd passed by the tunnel twice and stopped briefly to see if maybe he'd come out of it. There was no sight of him and they decided to keep going around the island. Smoke continued to rise from the valley. It looked threatening and it was hard for them not to think the worst, but nevertheless they pressed on. They would not give up until Damien was found.

Suddenly, Rufus heard something in the distance. He looked up and saw a helicopter coming close to the island. It was yellow and red and appeared to be some type of rescue helicopter. He could see that it was landing on the far side of the island, close to where the others were gathered. At any other time, this would have garnered his full attention, but for now, the search for Damien was their number one priority.

The boat rounded to the opposite side of the island from where their camp was located. It had been over a week since Captain Jones had driven a boat. This had been the longest stretch he'd ever gone without driving since he was a young teenage. The vessel was moving around twenty miles an hour and handled well. Though the mission was urgent, it did feel good to the captain to be back at the helm again. He was thankful he was able to help and use his abilities to help rescue his friend.

"Wait, slow down!" Rufus called out suddenly.

The captain slowed the motor and moved closer to the shore. Rufus didn't even wait until he was completely stopped, but rather jumped into the water while it was still a few feet deep and made his way toward the shore. He didn't want to wait because there coming out of the woods, he saw a young girl, and beside her he saw Damien. He was barefooted and stumbling as he walked. His shirt was burned at spots and badly torn. He looked like he'd been through a war, but overall Rufus was just thrilled to see him coming out of the woods from the valley. And not only by himself, but he had saved this last girl as well.

"Damien!" Rufus called out as he made it close to his employer.

"Hey, Rufus," he said, exhausted. He got down on all fours and started coughing. Between the smoke inhalation and running through the mountains, he felt sick. It took him a moment to gather himself. The rescued girl was beside him.

Captain Jones arrived close to them on the beach. "We have water," he said as he held out two bottles of water.

"Thanks," Damien said as he drank it down. The girl followed suit. Damien then poured some of the water on the backs of his hands that were burned.

"Are you ok?" Rufus asked, concerned.

Damien took a deep breath as he sat on the beach. He nodded his head before speaking. "Yeah, I got some burns on my hands and my neck. Hopefully they're only first or second degree."

"Um... yes, I don't think they look... too bad," Rufus said, trying to sound upbeat but failing miserably.

Damien turned to the young girl. "Are you ok? Did you get burned?"

She shook her head. "No, I'm fine," she responded with a slight smile.

"What happened in there?" Rufus asked.

Damien took another drink of water before speaking. "Well, I guess you saw that I led the men away from the boat."

"Yep, I saw that."

"Then I ran back to the warehouse place and tried to create a diversion, just in case some of the men weren't following me. So, I lit the warehouse on fire, hoping to get their attention."

"I would say you definitely got our attention," Jones added.

"Better yet," Rufus broke in. "A plane flew overhead after seeing the smoke, and even better than that, we just saw a rescue helicopter land close to our beach. We're being rescued!"

Damien just stared at Rufus as he said these words. They almost didn't sound real. *Being rescued.* It was like he couldn't grasp what that was like. They'd been on this island for over a week, constantly thinking about a boat or plane coming to their rescue, and now it didn't even seem real. Especially after everything he'd just been through, he couldn't believe it was over. He was going home.

Rescue boats from St. Kitts and Puerto Rico showed up on the island. A couple dozen rescue workers spread out onto the beach, helping in whatever manner they could, providing food and medical care. They worked quickly as they were concerned about the smoke billowing from the island's interior. Many of the rescue workers were amazed when they landed on the island. It was over a hundred miles northeast of Puerto Rico. No one knew that this island existed out here, and only one had heard of a passing rumor about the mysterious Shadow Island.

The helicopter began to lift off with Milo and Gladys on board. Overall, they were doing well medically, but being the most elderly of the group, as a precaution, the workers thought it was best to get them back to Puerto Rico as quickly as possible. Many tears were shed as the group waved goodbye, watching the helicopter fly away.

After caring for the people, the rescuers began loading everyone onto the boats. The residents of St. Kitts and Nevis would head back to those islands, while the Americans were going to Puerto Rico. A few goodbyes were said among the group as they were split up and put on the boats. They had all grown close during this time, and particularly going through the loss of Henry together made their bonds even stronger. Lifetime friendships had been established on the island.

The group was then struck with amazement as they heard the small shipping boat come toward them. They ran to the sides of their boats and were pleased to see Captain Jones and Rufus returning with Damien and another young lady. They were happy to see all of them, but more than anything, they were glad to see their leader return. It seemed only fitting that he was coming back with someone else he had saved.

The captain brought the boat close to the shore and the four exited. A handful of rescue workers met them on the beach, making sure they were initially fine. After taking a few minutes checking them over, the workers began to load them onto the rescue boats also. The fisherman Ron couldn't contain himself. He began clapping, showing his gratitude for Damien. Quickly all the others in the group followed suit, welcoming back their leader.

Damien couldn't help but smile. A tear rolled down his cheek. He was back with his people. Back with his friends.

Twelve hours had passed since the people were rescued from the island, and it was now the middle of the night. Lex Williamson had heard the report of the people being rescued and began quickly packing his belongings. The news hadn't reached the media yet, but he had inside connections. He figured that Damien or Rufus would probably let them know his location and that he was selling black-market goods. If there was any information concerning his whereabouts, the US government would spare no expense in tracking him down. He was currently located in a secret house in Nevis. He had stayed in Nevis for the past week conducting business and looking for Damien, Henry, and Rufus. Throughout the week he had many meetings with clients across the Caribbean. As of right now, he was regretting that decision to stay and wished he'd moved all his meetings.

One of his men knocked on the door. "Come in," Lex said.

The man opened the door. It was his driver. He was dressed professionally in a three-piece suit. "Sir, a boat has been prepared. We're planning to go south, maybe have a plane meet us in St. Lucia."

"Good," he said quietly. "The authorities will be looking for me on St. Kitts. We will need to stay far away."

"Yes sir, we found a spot where a private plane can pick us up and take us to Spain."

"Have you found a secured spot to land there?"

"Yes, we found a small airport that we were able…"

Williamson's man was suddenly stopped by loud shouting coming into the house. "Get down on the ground!"

The driver turned to see US soldiers entering the residence. He counted five of them coming toward him. They held their guns out, pointed toward him. He had no other options; he simply complied and dropped to the ground. A soldier was on him quickly.

Lex sat down on the bed. Time seemed to move slowly. There was nothing he could do. He was caught. He'd been running for so long, dodging the US government. He had lived under two different aliases, but now he was caught. Anger began boiling over inside of him. His sacred island was exposed, and his warehouse was burned to the ground. He was defeated. It wasn't long before the soldiers were on him and he was arrested.

Damien awoke in his hospital room in Puerto Rico. He was lying in bed, hooked up to IVs along with a heart rate monitor. Two days had passed since their rescue from the island. It was the middle of the afternoon. Doctors were watching him closely as he had breathed in a lot of smoke in the valley. They worried a little about his heart but were also treating the skin on the top of his hands. The doctors and nurses had taken great care of him and it seemed like every hour he was feeling better.

He had left a cable news channel on, and when he awoke, he wasn't surprised to see a news story about the island rescue. It had broken to the media in the middle of the morning the day before. Authorities had heard that one of the passengers had died and so they waited to make sure Henry's family were notified before word leaked out to the press.

Earlier in the day, he had seen a story about Lex Williamson and his arrest. There were also reports that the criminals who had been chasing Damien in the valley were also apprehended. The news station had done an extensive report about who Lex Williamson truly was and his business involvement with black-market goods. He was also linked with other crimes that had taken place across the country.

The news had now moved on to discuss the island and what had taken place on it. A live camera shot of the island appeared on the screen and it looked as if the fire had died out. Seeing the damage the fire had done made him extremely grateful that they had gotten all the children out alive. It brought him so much comfort knowing they were safe and no longer suffering in the darkness.

As more footage of the island flashed on the scene, Damien wondered about the island itself. The valley had made him extremely uneasy. He thought of the rumors associated with Lex Williamson and the island as a whole. The media did a thorough job reporting about Lex's beliefs, and how he dabbled with strange sorcery that went back to ancient times. The island had become a place where he would experiment with those beliefs. Damien still had lots of questions about everything. He would always wonder if there was truly a supernatural component to the island or if all the rumors and beliefs were simply a ruse to help Williamson hide his black-market goods. Whether any of this was true or not, what Damien did know was that the island was evil, and he wanted no part of it. Overall, he was thankful the island was exposed, the children were rescued, and that Williamson's black-market operations were shut down.

A quick knock sounded at his door. He didn't have time to respond before it opened. He was speechless as he saw his wife walk through the door. She had a big smile on her face. She was beautiful. "Damien!" she said with great joy.

"Julia!" he held out his arms as she ran to him. They embraced tightly, throwing aside any caution for the IVs or wires. Tears were flowing from both of them. She had flown out early this morning. Her plane had been delayed in a layover in Florida. It had greatly pushed back her arriving on Puerto Rico. The trip took her twice as long as usual and she also experienced a few delays as a couple of media outlets spotted her in the airport. But for right now, none of that mattered. She was with her husband. They were together.

"Let me look at you," she said, releasing Damien and gently placing her hands on the sides of his face.

"Oh, it's so great to see you, my love," Damien said with a big smile.

"You too," Julia squeezed him tighter. Her emotions were overflowing as she was so happy to see him. She thought of the last time she had seen him, and then thought about this day. There was a difference, such a great contrast. Even though he had been through an extremely difficult week, she would say he looked at peace. It was like a burden had been lifted from him. The shadow was gone.

Epilogue

Damien sat in the cafeteria and watched as the people passed by in a hurry. Two years had passed since he had been rescued from the island. Much had changed since he'd left. Now he found himself in a hospital again, except this time, the circumstances were much different. This was a time of joy.

He took a sip from the Styrofoam cup in front of him, and gently placed it down on the table. The individual across the table spoke, "Is it time to go back?"

Out of habit Damien looked down at his wrist. He smiled at himself as there was nothing there. He nodded slightly as he spoke quietly, "Yes... it's time to go back."

Damien stood to his feet and patted his daughter on the shoulder. Her name was Alexandria and she was twelve now. She was the same girl Damien had rescued from the valley when it was burning. She had been orphaned right before she was taken captive by Lex Williamson's men. When Damien and Julia heard about the history of this young lady and learned that she had no family to return to, they put in the effort to adopt her. It wasn't an easy road, but with the help of their state senator, they were able to adopt her three months after they left the island. Damien and Julia were both greatly pleased with how well she was making the transition.

Damien's work had also changed dramatically over the last two years. After Henry's death, he decided to sell the marketing business to two of his employees. He then started a new small business helping people with investments and managing of finances. The business was small, but it was steadily growing. Currently, he had three employees, one of which was a blond-haired guy from California named Beck.

Six months after the island rescue, Beck decided to take Damien up on his offer and come work with him. By that time, he was just starting his business of financial management. Beck started off small, doing office work for Damien, but he was a quick learner and Damien was able to give him more tasks. Beck's life had also changed in many other ways. He met a girl there in North Carolina and married her after four months of dating. Now a honeymoon baby was on the way. He was beyond happy about these changes in his life. And whenever his anniversary of being clean came around, Beck took time to celebrate.

Rufus, on the other hand, struggled greatly after leaving the island. His time in the valley particularly weighed heavy on him. He struggled with nightmares and depression, and couldn't hold down a job. Nine months ago, Damien had met with him and decided the best thing would be for him to get drastic help. Rufus agreed and relocated to Iowa where he moved in with Milo and Gladys. They were happy to help him work through the issues he was facing. Damien was pleased to see that just yesterday Milo had sent him an email saying Rufus was progressing well and was opening up more than he had in the last months. Damien could only hope this was a sign of good things to come.

The girl, Hope, along with the other children, were returned to their parents across the Caribbean, South America, and Europe. Most of them had only been gone from their families for a month. Hope had been separated the longest. Everyone from the island was extremely happy when they heard the news that her parents were located, and Hope was brought home.

The fisherman, Ron, and his son-in-law, Sean, returned home and continued to fish. Since being rescued, they had done many interviews about their time on the island. Ron had also written a book about the whole experience. It became an instant best-seller, and still is to this day. There are rumors a movie might be in the works. Damien kept in close contact with both of them. He considered them good friends.

Captain Jones went back to St. Kitts and started back with his business of captaining a ferry. His boat was towed back to St. Kitts where he had it fixed. *Captain Jones' Ferry Rides* became a popular tourist attraction for St. Kitts and Nevis. He was known for taking time with his passengers and telling stories of what it was like on the island. Currently, his rides were still popular, and it usually took a two-week advance reservation to get a spot on his boat.

The nurse Elizabeth continued to be an inspiration for her people in St. Kitts. When the story came out that she was once held captive as a young girl on Lex Williamson's island, it only added to people's admiration of her. She did a number of speeches and was now a representative in the government of St. Kitts. Her popularity spread to the United States as well, where she became a household name. At times she still struggled with Henry's death, but thankfully, Henry's family showed her great appreciation for the work she had done for him. It was the encouragement she greatly needed.

Ned and Damien became close after the island experience. Ned continued to show great remorse for the way he had acted. Damien was forgiving, and they had even met together a few times after they were rescued. Unfortunately, six months ago, Ned suffered a massive heart attack and passed away. It was a sad time, but all those from the island came together for the funeral. It was a strong show of support for Ned's family. In the midst of their sadness, the group made the most of it and enjoyed the reunion together. They would forever be close friends.

Damien and his adopted daughter, Alexandria, now took the elevator up to the fourth floor. It was where they had spent most of the morning as well as the day before, and it was where Julia was with their new baby. He was born in the early morning the day before. The labor had been quick and fairly smooth. Julia was now recovering and simply enjoying the new member of their family.

When they found out that they were having a boy, Damien and Julia both knew what his name should be... Henry. It was only appropriate after all Damien's friend and business partner had done for him over the years. Damien looked forward to telling his son about his name and the great man who had inspired it. His legacy would live on.

As they opened the door to the hospital room, Damien could see Julia holding little Henry. She had just finished feeding him. Alexandria quickly ran back to her mother's side. She couldn't get enough of her new baby brother. Damien sat on the edge of the bed by his wife's side. "How's he doing?" he asked.

Julia smiled as she held her son close. "He's fine. He's been doing well with his feedings."

"Great to hear," Damien said softly as he gently rubbed his son's head. Already he loved this little guy so much.

The road to having another baby wasn't easy. They suffered through a miscarriage in the first year back from the island, and when Julia was carrying Henry in her womb they often struggled with uncertain fears. Damien and Julia both had spent many evenings praying with Pastor Thomas about these struggles. He was a great help and encouragement through these trials of life.

As Damien now sat with his family, he thought of the hard road of losing Lucy and then the trial of the island. It definitely hadn't been easy, and at times he would still struggle with her loss. Nothing could ever replace Lucy and the memory of her would live on in Damien's mind forever. It was a memory of both sadness and joy.

A tear rolled down Julia's cheek as she admired her newborn son. "Damien, I just... love him so much."

Damien smiled as he looked at his son. "I do too, my love... I do too."

The journey of the last two years had been difficult, and Damien would admit that there were times when he had felt all alone. But, now, in this moment as Damien looked over his family and held them close, more than ever he knew that the Lord was his shepherd. He was leading Damien through life and walking close beside him ... just as He always had.

Also, check out these other titles from Tony Myers. Available at most online book distributors.

Singleton

"As someone with a lifelong interest in magic who has been fooling people as long as I remember, I love the chance to be fooled myself. As I read Singleton I was baffled. The first few pages of the book caught my attention just like the opening trick of a good magic show. From there I was kept in suspense as the mystery unfolded. Just when I thought it was impossible to tie together all the strange things which were occurring, Myers performs his best trick. In the last few pages of the book he brings the mystery to a satisfying yet shocking conclusion. Like a good magic show, Singleton leaves you wanting more. Fortunately, Myers has another book up his sleeve. If you are like me and enjoy a good mystery, then you may want to consider Stealing the Magic for yourself. If Singleton is any indication, it is bound to entertain and keep you in suspense."
   - John Neely, Magician

Stealing the Magic

"Myers delivers a page-turning mystery that grips the reader with its relatable characters and compelling plot. A taut, satisfying story for young suspense lovers and seasoned readers alike."

- Pamela Crane, literary judge and author of the award-winning *A Secondhand Life*

The Beauty of a Beast

"Nothing captivates an audience of all ages like knights, princesses, dragons, beasts and courage. The Beauty of a Beast proves that true. It is one of those books with a very familiar plot line, but an extreme twist at the end. While reading it, I was on the edge of my seat. Tony Myers does a fantastic job of capturing his audience's attention and not letting it go till the end of the book. Each character comes alive with every paragraph as their world becomes as real as ours. This clean, mind-blowing, nail-biting, easy-to-read book will have you eagerly turning each page and then anxiously anticipating the next book!"

- Aaron Moore

Made in the USA
Lexington, KY
01 December 2019

57911215R00164